BEAUTY AND THE ALIEN BEAST

GALAXY ALIEN WARRIORS

SEDONA VENEZ

WANT FREE SEDONA VENEZ BOOKS?

Sign up for Sedona Venez's Newsletter and receive FREE BOOKS. In addition to the free stories, you will also get special pricing, exclusive previews and news of new releases.

GET A FREE SEDONA VENEZ BOOK!

Join Sedona's mailing list to be the first to know of new releases, free books, special prices and other author giveaways.

https://sedonavenez.com/free-book

CHAPTER 1

ELLA

MY EYES SNAPPED open as I woke from the weirdest nightmare I had ever experienced in my life.

A moment later, I discovered I was in a cage. Pale metal bars, very shiny and set in a wide mesh pattern, surrounded me on five sides. The sixth was a narrow door and frame made from some thick, transparent material. The bottom, made of the same stuff, was on casters and seemed locked in place.

Oh God, what the fuck is this?

I was too uncomfortable for it to be a dream. My knees were tucked too hard against my full breasts. My belly, back, and shoulders ached stiffly.

My heart started to pound with terror, and it took all I had to keep quiet and not panic.

I've been kidnapped... but by whom?

Using the bars, I pulled myself to my feet and felt my joints crack from being balled up on the bottom of the cage. Seeing a small fold-down seat attached to the inside of the cage, I flipped it down, perching my ass on it uncomfortably, barely fitting a cheek and a half on the damn thing.

Fear died back a little as I caught my breath, eyes still blurry. I felt off-kilter.

Have I been drugged?

I looked down at myself and realized the tank top and fleece sleep shorts I remembered going to bed in were gone. Now I was dressed in a translucent cream-and-gold gown that accented my dark skin perfectly and clung to my ample curves. Beneath the dress was a gold harness that held up my large breasts, while a gold-belted loincloth matching the gown was the only thing that covered my ass —barely.

Shit. I've been kidnapped and turned into eye candy.

To make matters worse, I couldn't remember how I'd gotten here. My last clear memory was of dozing off under my fluffy comforter with an open book on my chest.

I gave myself a quick once-over. No injuries, but I could tell I'd been bathed, perfumed, and my thick, curly hair was now pulled back from my face, allowing the tendrils to tumble loose down my back. My nails were clean and gilded. My feet were bare, and someone had painted my toenails gold.

What the hell? I felt like an involuntary model in a lingerie show.

I looked out through the bars at a gleaming, well-lit space with a mirrored ceiling, shiny black floor, and walls made up entirely of flat-screen panels.

For a moment, I looked up at my reflection. I was covered in sparkly gold dust, with more of the glittery substance coating my lips and eyelids.

I focused back on the walls. Shimmering golden lettering in a language I didn't know scrolled across some of the panels, and other surfaces displayed scenes of a beautiful, pristine landscape. Drinking it all in, I tried to glean some information on where I was being held.

The scenes being shown on the walls didn't look like Earth.

My stomach plummeted.

The scape depicted towering, conical mountains and a purple-tinged sky set with a small blue-white sun. A cluster of four jewel-colored moons rode the track of a faint, shimmering Saturn-like ring. In the foreground, there was a shining city with slim towers composed of a reflective metal-like surface studded with multicolored lights. And a flock of heavy-bodied, alien-looking four-legged birds soared through the air.

My body shook, and the dizziness intensified.

Oh God... am I dreaming? Or... am I really on an alien world?

I shut my eyes, trying to gather my shattered memories.

Okay... think, Ella...

I remembered lying in bed at Mom's cabin upstate, where I'd come to enjoy one of the last warm weekends of the year. I had been sleepy from too many glasses of wine and a lot of good food, so I'd decided to go to bed earlier than usual. My mind locked on to those memories of normalcy.

I smiled slightly just thinking about Mom. Coming up to the cabin with her had done a lot to help me decompress from a long week of work in Manhattan. She and I had spent hours just sitting on the porch, talking and sipping wine while quietly regretting that summer had faded. We shared hilarious yet nostalgic stories about Dad, who had been gone three years now.

Of course, true to form, Mom had asked if I was happy being single. It had been the subtlest, most easygoing sort of pressure I was used to, so I didn't complain. Mom just didn't get why I hadn't dated in years, and she refused to accept my insistence that I just plain didn't have time.

At twenty-nine years old, I'd made my career a priority, and I didn't have time for the bullshit drama associated with dating in Manhattan. I had stopped looking for a Sunday-afternoon man in Saturday-night places. It didn't help that I was picky as hell and was simply exhausted of suited, thirtysomething men who were still trying to fuck everything that moved and wanted nothing to do with relationships. I wanted something "real" with a partner that was interested in me. A man I'd feel safe with at all times and who could accept me as is, not constantly trying to upgrade or improve me.

I closed my eyes, leaning against the bars, trying to remember more about last night. We had retired early, maybe nine o'clock. I sat up a while in my room, working on my curriculum for my next public health seminar—a presentation on the real effects of health care legislation in the Tri-State area over the last ten years. I'd drifted off with one of my reference books on my chest, still sorting facts and figures in my head.

My breath hitched when I recalled how I'd gotten here...

I was lying in bed, sleepy as hell, when a faint light shined through my bedroom windows. Yawning, I rolled away from the illumination, determined to grab some rest while I could.

The light got brighter.

I mashed my face into my pillow, desperately trying to get some sleep.

Then shit got so weird and scary when I was plucked right off the bed by some invisible force. I screamed, but there was no sound.

I tried to move my limbs, but I was paralyzed while my body floated through the air and right out the open second-story window.

My vision blurred from the bright glare before I felt a bruising pressure against my body, as though the energy were trying to skin me alive.

My heart raced as I screamed again, and again, there was no sound. The light flashed several times before I felt myself floating lower and lower until the force against my body released.

I was free... sort of.

I stared at my surroundings in disbelief.

This was my worst nightmare come true.

I was inside a tiny metal room with no doors.

On my hands and knees, I scuttled around like a cornered animal because there was no doubt in my mind what had just happened...

I'd been abducted by aliens.

CHAPTER 2

ELLA

THINK.

I dug the heel of my hand into my temple. *What happened next?*

I vaguely recollected waking up, groggy and bound to a floating gurney with two figures—aliens—flanking each side. The creatures were half my size and wore dark-gray matte jumpsuits. Each had different-colored skin—one gray, the other green—but they both had enormous heads with almond-shaped black eyes and a tiny mouth that emitted low, unrecognizable sounds every time it moved.

Am I remembering this right? Or is my mind playing tricks on me?

Frankly, I didn't know what was real anymore. Memories floated through my head in bits and pieces.

Did I really see the aliens puffing away on sticks that had glowed various colors while billowing drifts of pungently sweet mist? And did the green creature remove my earrings, replacing them with a pair of pale-gold disks?

Yes. That had to be real because as soon as the green alien clicked the small disks into place, the faint warbling sounds they made suddenly sounded like perfect English. And even though their voices were squeaky, like cartoon characters, I distinctly remembered their conversation...

"Is that one of the new model translators?" the gray alien asked the green one as I lay there listening, staring up at the mirrored surface of the ceiling that reflected the entire area of the room. I tried to move, but I was frozen in place and not in control of my body—they were.

The chain-smoking aliens continued chattering in bored tones like a couple of lab technicians.

The green alien replied, "Just the receivers. I'll have to put the Earthling back under for the throat unit. Let's give that a minute. She's still recovering from the last jolt we gave her."

My eyes tracked him in the shiny ceiling as he toddled across the cavernous lab to a work-table jutting from the wall and started poking around at the tools laid out on it.

"Uh, well... Oh, fish crap. Bellbucz? Where's the tranquilizer wand?"

The gray alien was named Bellbucz?

"You're the head med tech," Bellbucz snapped. "I don't touch your stuff. Where did you leave it this time, Varbec?" he asked before blowing an extra-large puff of vapor as he got up reluctantly.

"I don't know! Come help me. We're arriving at Planet Omers soon, and the earthling needs to be ready. They're starting to condition the new batch of humans tomorrow, and we need to make our quota."

Humans?

Alarm flooded my system. I wanted to scream... fight... run away... but I couldn't do anything but lie there immobile due to whatever they did to keep me stationary.

"All right. All right," Bellbucz answered before joining Varbec. "Are you sure you cali-

brated the human's new translator unit correctly?"

"*Of course. The earthling is worthless if she can't understand her new owner's commands.*"

My new owner? Oh sweet baby Jesus... the aliens are trafficking humans—aka earthlings—and I'm going to be sold like cattle.

Varbec continued. "My mate just birthed twenty hungry younglings. And if I don't get paid, I can't buy food, which means they'll eat me instead."

"*You wouldn't be the first Reticulan to get eaten by your younglings,*" Bellbucz replied at little too matter-of-fact.

"*Quiet, fool!*" Varbec barked. "*We'll get paid if we configure her correctly. She's a prime mating vessel... the kind that will go straight to the Omers for conditioning, then sold to the Wulfaen Gladiators to rut with.*"

Mating vessel? Conditioning? And what the hell is a Wulfaen Gladiator?

Bellbucz hissed, "I almost feel sorry for the weak humans. The four-armed Gladiators are brutal, disgusting, and hideous when they shift into their furry beasts."

I swallowed hard. Four arms? Furry beasts?

"I agree," Varbec said. "But at least they don't fuck their females in beast form, which we can't say about the Omers." He snorted. "A sexual mating with the horned Omers would kill the females very painfully. The hard shell at the tip of their staff would tear the females apart inside. They would bleed out, and the pain would be excruciating. I wouldn't even wish it upon an enemy."

My stomach rolled with panic.

Bellbucz nodded slowly. "The Earthlings are lucky that our physical exam of the first human female we abducted confirmed they are not capable of breeding with the Omers or giving them sexual relief."

Varbec replied, "It is good that we finally convinced the idiot Omers that since the Gladiators no longer have females, the human slaves might be worth something to the Wulfaen."

"The slaves might be the key to saving the Gladiator race from extinction," Bellbucz retorted. "Which means more pay for us. Too bad we still can't cut the Omers out of the transaction and do business directly with the Gladiators ourselves."

"I am working on a way," Varbec answered. "But it will take time to get an audience with the alphas of the Gladiators. My sources tell me there is conflict among the Gladiators on whether they should buy the earthlings. Some nonsense about them not wanting to force the humans into mating with their males." He paused. "They are a proud race... Too proud, if you ask me, given that they're facing eventual extinction if they don't find a race of females to breed with their Gladiators."

Bellbucz laughed before saying, "Barbaric idiots."

"Yes, they are," Varbec conceded. "Even when their own attempts to find suitable females from other alien races have proven fruitless, they still hesitate to buy the humans."

"Maybe that is why they hesitate," Bellbucz said, "because they don't think the humans are the answer to their problem."

"It doesn't matter," Varbec snapped. "Our data shows that at least the earthlings are sexually compatible with the Gladiators, so they can pass them around to their males for rutting."

Fear struck me deeply.

"Gladiators don't share their females," Bellbucz said.

Varbec snapped, "Desperate times sometimes call for desperate measures."

I heard something else being jostled around, then Varbec said, "Let's get back to the matter at hand—getting this female ready. The calibration is fine on the receivers. These humans have simple auditory centers in those squishy little brains of theirs. I'm just worried the impatient Omers will forget to install the right power crystal once we deliver her. They've done it twice already. The wrong one will slowly fry the circuits, and then she will not be able to communicate with the male she ends up with."

They both came back over, dragging some huge cart with them.

"Don't we have a purple-grade crystal here?" Bellbucz started searching through the cart.

"No. That's the problem with the sudden huge demand for female earthlings. The Omers are greedy and are ordering them too *fast, but they don't pay us enough up front, so we always run out of supplies." Varbec's voice dripped with resentment. "I can't wait to get to Planet Omers so we can get paid."*

I must have drifted off in the middle of their strange conversation because I didn't remember anything after that. But now, mulling over the aliens' dialogue, I touched my throat and felt a small tender spot just over my voice box.

This is it. This is real. I've been abducted by aliens.

And I'm going to be "conditioned" by horned aliens called "Omers" and then forced to have sex with "Wulfaen Gladiators" who turn into furry beasts.

Fuck. My. Life.

I was terrified but had to keep my shit together to cope with the situation and figure out a way back home.

Glancing around the room, I thought it was strange that I was alone in a space that was so huge my cage took up very little of it. And then there were all the images on the walls of an awe-inspiring alien world.

Am I already on Planet Omers? And can I survive here if I manage to escape? Eat the food? Breathe the air?

As I stared at the shifting images, one thing I noticed was the huge swaths of wilderness between the shining cities, trees the size of skyscrapers and bizarre vegetation. And here I was, a city girl born and bred, with absolutely no experience in wilderness survival.

But I was getting ahead of myself. First, I had to escape and then figure out a way back to Earth.

My first objective was to find out who the hell the Omers and Wulfaen were and then show them they'd messed with the wrong damn woman. My second was to negotiate my freedom, which seemed like a long shot at best. In any event, I wasn't going down without a fucking fight. And I was going to survive and find a way out of here.

My head snapped in the direction of the door that opened across the showroom. A whole panel of the wall simply slid aside, letting in a pair of very tall figures. They were speaking to each other in rumbling, musical voices with a faint, unfamiliar accent.

I tensed as they approached.

More aliens. A different species this time.

Both had blue skin and were gigantic, broad-shouldered with four arms, one pair set beneath the other, ending in broad, thick-fingered hands. Their strong-featured, high-cheekboned faces looked almost human, except when they spoke, sharp teeth flashed behind their lips. One had golden eyes, the other orange. Both males wore a sort of close-fitting dark-gray armor of some leathery-looking stuff that left their arms bare save for sheaths covering their forearms. They both had pointed ears and two large bull-like jet-black horns protruding from their heads.

So... these must be the Omers.

CHAPTER 3

TEKEN

IT WAS the tenth day of the fifth month—just as the blooming season was ending—and I was late for my urgent meeting with my pack elders, the oldest Gladiators who preserved pack history and guided us with their knowledge.

The warm air blew against my skin as I stepped outside my quarters and strode down the dirt path that sliced through several rows of large stone-façade dwellings.

It was quiet, the distant sounds of Gladiators drifting to me as I continued along the pathway and through the central courtyard with a practice arena that we used to train our riding dogs. A few Gladiators were milling around, and all inclined their heads to me with one word of greeting. "Alpha."

I responded, "Gladiator," to each while traversing away and exiting the courtyard that faced a short road leading to our massive arena, the ruin where our ancestors had once fought as slaves and had become the symbol of our reborn order of the Wulfaen Gladiators.

Finally, inside the arena, I quickly made my way across the ground and stepped through the opening that would lead me deep within, past pens where my forefathers had slept, bled, and had sex with their mates.

Journeying by the memorials of ancient skulls perched on the hilts of equally ancient swords, each blade driven into the rock of their former prison, I finally reached the council chamber, deep in the underground crypt where the most honored of our ancestors were buried.

Surrounded by niches full of skulls, five ancient elder Gladiators stood, talking and gesturing animatedly. They all had shaved heads and long beards, and their sleeveless black robes rustled as they argued.

Their voices quieted when I entered, and

they stood at attention, acknowledging me with, "Greetings, Alpha Teken."

I rumbled back, "Elders," before storming over to my stone throne and sitting. "So? What's the purpose of this meeting?"

"We've received word from the alphas from sectors one and two," the elder of peace said solemnly as he tugged his pure-white beard.

His eyes were an unusual dark blue-green, which I had inherited. He was the oldest, and despite his position, he was still the most skilled and powerful warrior among them. He was also my grandfather and guardian, and I called him by his first name, Joanor.

"Both had to hunt and kill several of their Gladiators who succumbed to the mating sickness, sending their Wulfaen feral. Elders from both sectors suspect that we do not have long before the sickness spreads throughout the Gladiator race." He glanced at each elder, who nodded in turn. "And we all agree."

At his words, I shuddered. The sickness was what all Gladiators feared. It was a fate worse than death. And if we could not find some way to fix the female shortage, I would find myself in that very situation much sooner than I was willing to admit.

I'd never witnessed the sickness, but I'd heard enough tales of it from my grandfather. When the void of not having a *sheleki*—mate—could no longer be contained, it consumed a Gladiator from the inside out, forcing his Wulfaen—the inner beast—to take over, locking the Gladiator within his animal. At will, all males could shift forms—from Gladiator to Wulfaen and back—and prided themselves for having control over their Wulfaen. But when the sickness consumed them, the beast was in charge, sending both Gladiator and Wulfaen feral.

The elder of ethics stepped forward before saying, "Alpha, we still do not know why the sickness is attacking the younger males as opposed to the elders. But tensions are high within sectors one and two. That is why they voted for buying the earthling females from the Omers."

"Elder," I hissed, "I've made my opinion on this matter clear."

Ethics replied, "Yes. You have. But it is our duty to inform you of the facts, whether you agree with the outcome or not."

I waved my hand. "Proceed."

Ethics continued. "According to the Omers, the female earthlings are sexually compatible with our males and are capable of bearing our pups. Everything that I've said has been confirmed by our medics, so this is fact." He pursed his lips before finishing. "This is why sectors one and two would like to reconvene the council."

I snapped, "Why?"

"They would like you to reconsider your vote," he answered.

I shook my head. "They would have had better luck begging the alphas from sectors four and five to change their votes."

The elder of ethics replied, "They did, but sectors four and five refused to change their stance. And since you were the deciding vote, sectors one and two are demanding that you see reason and side with them."

The elder of logic interjected, "Our alpha is reasonable. They are not. What they are attempting to do is circumvent the council's process." He rubbed his chin. "The Council of Five was created by our ancestors to prevent such a thing from happening. Our law is resolute. Each alpha has a vote, and the consensus wins."

Since that was blatant fact, none of us replied.

Many moons ago, our ancestors joined together under the leadership of five alphas—descendants of the royal Wulfaen Gladiator bloodline—who led all Gladiators into battle and freedom from the Omers.

In the wake of the war, the alphas returned to tribal ways and created five packs, each with their own alpha who ruled his own sector with absolute control and an iron fist. But not too long after, war and strife arose between the alphas.

Following centuries of bloodshed and death, the alphas decided to draw up a treaty that was satisfactory to each. As a result, the Council of Five was formed, made up of one alpha from each pack, who would meet—on neutral territory—to discuss politics, business, and other issues related to keeping the Wulfaen Gladiators in harmony. As the leader of one of the largest packs and sectors, I held one of the five seats on the council.

"Well, you can send word that my vote is unchanged," I answered. "My decision is still no to buying earthlings from the Omers for mating and breeding."

How far have we fallen as a society that we have let desperate straits push us into this state of moral compromise?

"I understand that one of my many duties as alpha is to ensure that my pack survives, but to condone slavery?" I arched a brow. "No! That I will never agree with."

"I've made my opinion on this matter clear," the elder of foresight said. He was the youngest and most muscular, with a trimmer, gold-hued beard and dark-purple eyes. "Relying on the Omers for females is foolish. Many solar cycles ago, we were once their slaves and fought a bloody battle to win our freedom. Now I believe the Omers's offer to sell us the one thing that we need to survive is just another way to force us back into servitude."

I nodded in agreement. It wasn't long ago that all Gladiators were once the Omers's property. The vile Omers treated us like wild animals, forcing us to remain in our beast form—the Wulfaen—fighting other alien races for the Omers's entertainment, coins, and territory. Most of the Gladiators went feral because it was not good for us to remain in our beast form for too long, allowing our animal to take control of our mind. When we went feral, we were slaughtered like animals. But the most damning part of our enslavement was that the Omers used our females for fucking, their staffs ripping into our females, killing most. Those that survived became weak and sick, incurring a very slow and painful death.

"Alpha." The elder of war held up his hand. "The truth of the matter is that Gladiators from all sectors—including ours—are restless. They need to find their one true mate... their sheleki." He paused. "None of the nearby planets that we've visited have females who are capable of bearing our younglings. We've exhausted all logical solutions."

This was true. Many Gladiators—including me—had visited nearby planets in search of our sheleki, to no avail. Most females that we'd encountered weren't sexually compatible.

War continued. "It is unwise to ignore the fact that earthlings will remedy the sexual unease among the Gladiators. This could slow the spread of the mating sickness."

I could attest to the hardship of not having a soft female of my own to care for and protect, but there was a limit to how far I'd go to attain my mate. I was among the many who believed that someday the gods would provide willing mates for all my fellow brethren. When that day came—and it would—Gladiators were ready to prove themselves worthy of claiming and mating our chosen female.

Despite the fact that none of the younger Gladiators—like me—had ever experienced rutting with a non-simulated female, we were armed with a wealth of knowledge on how to satisfy our mate. As a rite of passage, all males were sent to the nearby planet Jupiter to learn the art of pleasing our future female from the VRCMB—virtual reality celestial mating simulator. The fully interactive tech system taught us all the skills required to stimulate her sexual chamber while planting our seed in a manner that would eventually result in her belly becoming round with our pup.

"I've made my opinion clear," I growled. "I will never agree or condone the act of forcing females to give us pleasure. Any sexual contact between the earthlings and us must be consensual." I eyed each and every one of the elders. "We are proud warriors and do not need to resort to forcing our needs on females."

Left to myself, I would have ridden into the complex and rescued every one of those females—earthlings and other races—after making the slavers pay for their wickedness with blood.

"I agree with Alpha," the elder of logic said. "But we have a big problem. Thirty orbits have passed since a youngling was born to our people. Thirty."

He spoke of me, the last Gladiator born, the son of an alpha elder from the royal bloodline. I had been born to a surrogate from donated ova and my father's essence, and then I was taken back to my sector to be raised and trained in our ways.

"We are running out of solutions to prevent our race from extinction. Our surrogate program only produced males, and interplanetary visits resulted in no females of breeding compatibility. We need to find females for our Gladiators to claim and mate, and despite the unseemly proposition of buying earthling females from the Omers, that seems to be our only solution for survival."

"All of our solutions have failed because of one"—I held up a finger—"simple truth. Our mating cannot be forced. Our Wulfaen chooses our sheleki, and only that match allows us to breed strong female pups."

In order to survive, our Wulfaen needed to find the perfect mate, a female destined for us alone, whose soul resonated with our Wulfaen and whose body and mind and heart were a perfect match for our own. When a Gladiator meets his mate, he is subjected to a type of frenzy. It overtakes the mind and the body, and the Gladiator in question runs only on instinct.

I continued. "But slavery is not going to happen. That is why I must convince the council that encouraging open contact with the earthling females is a better plan to bolster our fertile female population than buying them from the slavers." I paused, eyeing them with a hard stare. "I've heard that the Omers ill-treat the females, and that is not our way. So the first step of my plan is scouting the slave trainers' facility. We must have evidence of how badly the females are being treated. Then I will convene the council, reporting our observations, and put forth a vote for a joint pack mission to attack the facility, freeing all the females and shutting down the slavers for good."

My pack could easily go it alone to the Omers's facility, slaughtering the slavers and freeing the females, but the Omers would declare war against all packs. I couldn't let my actions affect my brothers when they had no hand in my decision. Besides, it wasn't in my nature to go against council law, which stated that all decisions that could put our entire race in jeopardy or incite war must be voted on by the council.

I continued. "Once all females are freed and are teleported back to their planet, we will strategize on defeating the Omers in the war they will surely incite against us."

"And what will we do about the earthlings?" the elder of logic asked. "Our teleport chambers are incapable of sending them back to Earth. And the Reticulans cannot be trusted."

I answered, "We will offer the earthlings asylum and protection under the council's authority."

"That is a fair and just plan," Joanor mused as he tugged his white beard. "But how will we determine where they shall live? All packs will want to offer safe harbor to the earthlings, and fighting will ensue for that right. I suggest the females visit each pack and make their own determinations about which sector is suitable."

"Finally, we're getting somewhere!" The elder of war rolled his shoulders, then turned to me. "Who from our pack will you send on this mission?"

"I will go," I answered. "I need to see for myself the conditions of the slave facility. I will go in the guise of a noble from another planet that is interested in buying a female."

All five pairs of eyes turned to me, and the elders nodded in agreement.

"Then it's settled," I said before standing. "I will go to my chambers and prepare." I stared at my grandfather. "Have a Gladiator bring me the proper clothes and gear for my disguise," I said before walking away.

CHAPTER 4

TEKEN

AFTER MY MEETING with the elders, I was back inside my home that was once the estate of a wealthy elite slaver.

As the alpha of my pack, I was allotted the largest home. The expansive space had multiple rooms, including servant quarters, courtyard, bath, pool, storage room, garden, and an exercise facility. Each room was high-ceilinged, longish, and narrow, like a trio of hallways. The farthest one in was my meditation chamber.

I was proud of my home and had covered the stone walls in pale air-hardening plaster and laid down a dark-green carpet. Bowls of glow fish provided light, and I fed them some dried shrimp to get them shining brightly, checking their water while I did. But time was of the essence, so I strode up to the mirror, the only decoration aside from the rack for my weapons sitting in front of it, and considered myself as I removed the trappings that identified me as a Gladiator.

The earrings that represented our status as freed slaves went into the tray atop the weapon rack. I couldn't do anything about my close-cropped hair, which was only worn by non-elder Gladiators, but I presumed my brethren would bring me a hairpiece of some sort. I ran my hand through the silvery strands and then removed my metal bracers and set them on the tray as well.

No point in shedding my dark-gray iron-skin armor—no male in his prime went without it in public—but I removed the decorations that showed the honors I had achieved among my people. My medals, the amulet at my throat, even my rings.

Today, I lay aside the trappings of who I am to do what a Gladiator of honor must do.

I hated slavery as much as the rest of my brethren. Now the Gladiators were allowing the practice of slavery to crop up in another form and excusing it as biological necessity. But we could handle the matter of finding mates for our people without degenerating ethically by centuries in the process.

I was unmated, like all males of my race. And the lack of females made Gladiators more aggressive since we were very sexual by nature, and most of us—including me—felt the frustration of not having a female to mate.

In order to survive, our males needed to find a sheleki. The primal want was as natural and necessary as breathing. Our perfect female was destined for us alone. When a Gladiator found his one true mate, he felt an unavoidable need to bind with her, planting our seed and watching her grow heavy with a youngling. It meant providing for our family, risking life and limb to ensure their safety.

Something deep inside me ached at the thought. I longed for the softness of a mate. A female I could cherish and protect—and a pup I could guide and teach.

The last thing I removed—very reluctantly—was my sword. It had been passed down for three generations, and I rarely went anywhere without it. But visiting alien nobles from other planets did not wear swords. They preferred energy weapons, which could stun or kill at the wiggle of a finger, requiring no skill or courage at all.

I disdained such weapons, but I was skilled with them. And I refused to visit the slavers unarmed, especially since I would have to trek through the jungle to get there. If I used the arena's teleport chamber to travel to the slavers' complex, it would identify my origin point and my cover would be blown.

A tap on my outer door alerted me that a pack member had arrived with my disguise. I decided I would ride out immediately. The sooner I gathered evidence of the crimes being committed against the females, the sooner the females would be freed. And in my opinion, their freedom was all that mattered.

CHAPTER 5
ELLA

"SMILE, EARTHLING," my bull-horned captor instructed in a syrupy voice while his fists clenched around a crystal pain stick. "You do not smile enough." The scar tissue that stretched across his skin pulled the side of his mouth into a permanent smirk that I desperately wanted smack away.

"How about you hop in this cage in my place and tell me how much you feel like smiling, you bull-horned freak?" I snapped.

Fuck you, asshole alien. You can make me bleed, but you cannot break me.

I didn't know his name, and he hadn't asked for mine. All I knew was this overseer was even bigger than the other Omers I'd seen so far.

He smiled, stepping a little closer to the bars of my cage before running his thumb over what he called the pain stick. I barely had time to brace for impact before my body started to lock up and waves of agony jolted up my spine. But I forced myself to stay on my feet.

He turned up the power. My knees shook, forcing me to brace myself against the wall as the pain raced through my veins. Logically, I knew this torture was just remote nerve stimulation, but it felt like my spine was being yanked out of my body.

Fuck! Fuck! Oh God, Ella—no, don't start crying. Don't scream. Don't give him the fucking satisfaction!

I held on and held on and held on, while his scowl deepened and he turned up the dial on the pain stick.

"Stubborn female. Don't you know this could kill you?" He never ceased to be shocked at my pain tolerance.

Finally, he deactivated the stick.

I sagged against the bars, wheezing with every breath I took.

He stared at me wide-eyed. "Is it your desire to die, human? Is that it? If you do not learn compliance, you will be euthanized."

"Do it," I hissed. "Put me out of my misery. I'd rather die than shame myself and my mother by turning into some smiling, compliant little 'hostess.'"

"Stupid earthling!" He snarled before activating the pain stick again.

I doubled over, feeling the energy punch against my stomach as though I'd been hit by a boxer fighting for a championship belt. I gagged, determined to avoid vomiting my last meal. But he just kept increasing the pain, which felt like a spiked baseball bat pummeling my body.

Growling in frustration, he cut off the pain stick again.

I was shaking all over and bathed in sweat, but I still met his gaze when he locked eyes with me.

"What madness afflicts you, earthling?" he demanded.

I smirked at him through the bars. "Go ahead. Hit it again. Knock me out. Make me shit myself. All you're doing is fueling my hate fire, asshole."

I didn't know how many days and nights had gone by since I'd been brought to this place. Very little changed day to day, and the bland beige slop they fed me showed up irregularly. I suspected they were trying to disorient me. Sometimes the food arrived only when I had been starving for hours, but occasionally, they brought the slop while I was still digesting the last serving of the tasteless mess.

And my cage became an uncomfortable home they kept me in for hours without fail. The only time I was permitted to leave was after every meal when they took me to a small white cubicle with a squat toilet and handheld shower. There I could take care of my bodily needs and clean myself up. Right now, my death grip on the bars was the only thing keeping me upright, and I knew the sweat would itch once it dried on my skin. I craved one of those showers, but I wasn't about to kiss his ass to get it.

The overseer frowned. "The longer you fight, the longer your conditioning period and the more you get tortured. Give in, human. Accept your fate, and things will go better for you."

Oh, really, asshole? You want to feed me

that line of bullshit? I know you'll torture me either way because you like it. There are guys like you on Earth... I know the type.

I smiled sweetly up at him, which made his brow knit in confusion. He bent a little closer to me, examining my face. Then in a low, intimate voice, I said simply, "Go fuck yourself."

"I'll break you. This I swear," he barked before stomping out of the space.

Alone, I let my knees buckle and fell onto my cage floor. The pain from being tortured had left me nauseated and exhausted, but I hung on to my emotional strength. I would survive, and no amount of torture was going to break me. They could continue their abuse, but I'd still cling to my free will.

"Girl, you are crazy," came a voice from my left.

Turning my head, I glared at the tiny, athletic woman with a Los Angeles accent who watched me knowingly from inside her own cage. She had the same gold translator disks hooked into the lobes of her small ears.

"Don't you know they have a time limit on how long they'll put up with your shit? He isn't kidding about euthanizing you if you won't get with the program."

During my stay, the room had slowly filled with other kidnapped human women. There were maybe a dozen of us now, of all ethnic backgrounds. From the looks of it, we varied slightly in age. And we were all dressed in assorted colors of weird alien lingerie, which ranged from flattering to stripper-embarrassing.

Fucking horny-ass aliens are collecting us like exotic human sex dolls.

I grumbled, "I'm not afraid of those aliens," while pulling myself into something resembling a sitting position. I shoved my hair off my face, still trying to catch my breath from my exhausting torture session. "How long have you been here?"

"I have no fucking idea," L.A. accent answered. "I was going shopping when they grabbed me. Shopping!" She huffed. "I've got the worst luck ever." She paused. "One minute I'm in a big-box store at three in the morning, looking for cheap wine. The next, I'm here... in a damn cage like some animal. Fuck! My boyfriend's definitely going to think

I ditched him." The woman's rosebud lips twisted.

"I can't keep track of time," I interjected. "I think they keep us indoors and away from clocks and windows and vary when they feed us so we can't figure it out." I hated it. It disoriented me and left me feeling permanently exhausted and queasy. But I was determined to survive until they slipped up, giving me an opportunity to escape.

I've got to get back home to Mom or, at the very least, get word to her that I'm alive. Knowing her, she's in a panic over my disappearance.

I swallowed hard, blinking back the tears that threatened to fall.

I have a family, a job, and a damn life to return to—even if it's boring as hell and my romantic life ain't shit.

"Yeah, it's like Abu Ghraib with lingerie," another prisoner growled under her breath. "Except with more purpose. They basically keep up this same shit until we either decide to get with their damn alien program or we wash out and they kill us. This shit is crazy. Those fucking aliens keep the pressure on by never telling us when our number's up. But I guarantee you they'll kill you right in front of the rest of us to scare the shit out of everybody."

"What is the point of all this?" I asked.

Another woman chimed in. "I heard them talking about something called a 'fertility rating.' Like they're planning to breed us or something. I also heard they have several types of females from other alien planets. They're segregating us by alien race. That's why all the humans are in here—something about it being easier for them to condition us."

Other alien females? Fertility rating? Breeding? Forced sex—and motherhood on top of it? I shuddered with revulsion. *I refuse to be some alien's baby mama.*

"Oh, hell no..." I muttered while I rubbed the spot on my neck where one of the Omers had embedded an implant that he said I needed to survive. Without the device, I wouldn't even be able to breathe the air outside this place.

The woman shrugged. "Yeah, well, apparently, the Omers are going to sell us to some four-armed alien called a Wulfaen Gladiator. I heard the Wulfaen thingy can shift into a huge mutant wolf—like in one of those block-buster horror movies."

"Holy shit," I whispered.

"According to the rumor spreading around, that's not the most horrifying part," the woman added. "The Wulfaen want to impregnate us with their furry babies because they're dying from some sickness. When I heard that info, I shit on myself... literally."

I groaned. "This has to be some fucked-up dream."

The woman snorted. "Girl, every day since I woke up in this hellhole, I've been clicking my heels and chanting, 'There's no place like home,' hoping I'd magically transport myself back to Earth... But look... I'm still here. In this darn cage." She sighed heavily. "By the way, my name's Sheryl."

"Ella," I replied, my mind spinning, trying to piece together all the information I'd learned.

So the Omers plan to brainwash our asses and sell us as sex slaves to four-armed shapeshifting Wulfaen Gladiators who plan on knocking us up with their mutant babies?

This can't be happening.

But it is... and this planet is my new reality.

And now I was more determined than ever to escape, or I was going to get fucked—in more ways than one—by those damn Wulfaen Gladiators.

CHAPTER 6

TEKEN

BY THE TIME I reached the luxury suite the slavers kept for their paying guests, my riding dog Brax and I were both exhausted.

I hopped off his shaggy black back, and Brax shook himself, baring a double row of teeth in an enormous yawn. Domesticating the huge but loyal carnivores wasn't easy and neither was bonding with them, but they were indispensable in the trackless jungle.

One week of riding, traversing rivers, and fighting through the wild and untamed vege-tation had left me with a few new scars, but nothing serious. Brax had at least eaten well on the dead we left. As for me, I had found myself brooding far too much in my quiet moments as I thought about the slavers and the frightened alien females they "processed" at our destination.

Gladiators like me had a strong sense of right and wrong. But right now, as I pretended to be a wealthy noble visiting from another planet, with a taste for conditioned alien females, my high morals could be a liability on this mission.

Striding over to the edge of the clearing around the property, I found a little alcove to clean up and adjust my disguise. The temporary, jaw-length wig of dark-silver hair had been bonded to my scalp before I had left home. I used a nanite bathing cloth on myself and my armor and a grooming brush on Brax, then unsealed the dustproof, waterproof packet with the rest of my concealment inside of it. A short cloak and sleeveless tunic were a dark sea blue, and a set of jeweled rings and armbands replaced my bracers. Once I was dressed, I put my travel clothes into the packet and buried it. I clipped a dummy compliance collar on Brax, scratched his floppy ears, and stepped out into the open.

The complex was surrounded by heavy, dull metal walls studded with defensive weapons and sensor arrays. Several of the arrays oriented my direction as I walked up to the tall, arched front gate that was guarded by two well-dressed mercenaries with long white braids.

"The dog is only allowed in with a compliance collar on at all times," the shorter one needlessly said in a gravelly voice. One of his arms was a mere stump and another was missing a few fingers. I wondered if he had been punished for disloyalty or had simply been unlucky on a slave-catching mission. Either way, I had no sympathy for him.

"I'm aware," I said in a haughty voice. "I'm coming off a two-week vacation, hunting in the wilds of Neptune, and I'm interested in procuring a female. I want to see what you've got." My skin crawled just saying the words.

The other mercenary bowed and said, "Very well...?"

"I am Lord Nadaris," I replied. "You will find me in the Capitol Interplanetary Registry." And he would, thanks to a false identity that had been inserted into the registry years ago for my use during my frequent interplanetary travel on Gladiator business.

The mercenary nodded, pulling out a

small computube, unreeling the screen from a slit in its side, and setting to work looking up my name. The registry would tell him that Nadaris's net worth was roughly twice that of the average lord. I saw his eyebrows rise and knew it had sunk in. I was an adventurous, perpetually bored noble with money to burn, who might bring home a whole harem.

He closed the device and coughed politely, tucking away the tube. "Very good, Lord Nadaris. We will prepare a complimentary suite for you, and then you can view our offerings. It is a bit early in the season for training. Most of the new hostesses are not fully conditioned."

"Please. It's not a problem. Besides, I like my females with a bit more spirit, if you know what I'm saying." I winked and nudged both males with a chuckle. "At any rate, that will be satisfactory. Remember that the dog will require a significant game meat allowance. Otherwise, he may eat one of your men." I said this very lightly, and this time, both glanced at Brax nervously.

"Of course, milord." They pushed open the tall doors for me, and I strode inside with Brax at my heel.

CHAPTER 7

TEKEN

A WHILE LATER, I left Brax napping on the second bed in the suite, his belly full of griff meat, and went out to explore the pleasure house.

It didn't take long for word to get around that a wealthy noble was visiting and looking to buy a female. Suddenly, my wine cup was always filled, my plate always had some new delicacy landing on it, and nosy and groveling slavers were asking all sorts of questions about my sexual preferences.

Manar, an oily little man with sparse hair, was the pushiest among the inquirers, introducing himself as the chief of staff in this place, second only to their leader. "We have three of our four races available today. Nalian, Xerxian, and earthling. All of them are lightly conditioned now. However, making them available for our male guests is often an integral part of their programming. You may try up to four of our current stock, free of charge."

I wanted to rip out his throat for talking about females in such a degrading manner. They should be treated with respect, honored and adored, especially when my people would go extinct without them.

I forced my lips up into a smile even as the cloak of sadness settled into my bones. I ached to find my mate. A female that I could cherish and protect. For a pup that I could guide and teach. Sometimes it felt like I would go feral without the soft touch of a mate. Yet, instead of treating these earthlings like the genetic saviors of our race, we were treating them as commodities.

This isn't right.

I wanted to lash out violently, but there was a mission to complete. "And how do you ensure compliance to your visitors if the females are only half conditioned?"

"We use Darsis Vine—the purest extract." He grinned. "It simulates the mating frenzy with no ill side effects. Just a euphoric and *very* enthusiastic bed warmer, who will also be highly suggestible for the duration." He poured me more golden wine from a fluted crystal decanter.

"That sounds most promising." I nodded.

I wasn't worried about the ramifications of drinking the concoction—I had taken a counter-intoxicant before emerging from my room. Playing along with the fool, I continued to drink the good wine enthusiastically, re-membering to loosen my manner as if intoxi-cated while he kept refilling. I had more than enough detox sprays in the vials hidden in my belt.

I pondered the scrolling screens that ran around the top half of the walls. Images of beautiful, seminude alien females should have stirred my cock, but the knowledge that every one of them was here against her will damp-ened my arousal. I examined the images care-fully—the ebony-skinned Xerxians with their iridescent eyes and cottony hair, so lithe and slim and nimble fingered. The blue, lush-bodied Nalians with curves for days. I was informed the Taurian hostess slaves were rare and expensive—not because there weren't a lot of attractive ones, but because they were the hardest to catch and train and the most dangerous if they broke out of captivity. But Manar was quick to tell me that the violent, vividly colored amphibians had amazingly strong sex drives.

When the images of females that I'd never seen popped up on the scrolling screens, Manar boasted about the earthlings—humans, they called themselves. According to him, the earthlings were the most diverse race, with differing body types, skin, hair, and eye colors. They were supposed to be sexually compatible with very few aliens and have nurturing qualities and combat readiness that varied tremendously across a variety of cultures and subraces. Aside from a basic form of hair—on both their head and body—they had only two arms, two breasts, an omnivorous diet, and a high orgasmic capacity. Curiously, no human female displayed on the screens looked much like the next.

The humans were fascinating. Unlike the other three races, who knew of our existence at least in passing, humans had no idea that we existed—or that any other space-faring race existed. Yet they also showed the most likelihood of approaching and attempting to interact with a nonhuman.

I needed to speak to one of the humans. Maybe they would be willing to give me inside information on this place. It worried me that I had never interacted with any of the earthlings, but I decided to give it a try.

"I would like to see the humans," I said calmly. "Please take me to their display room immediately."

CHAPTER 8

ELLA

SOMETHING WAS wrong with my translator. It kept cutting out midsentence, sometimes mid-word. It stayed off for just a second or two at first, but as the day went on, it cut out longer and longer until I was hearing an elaborate, purring language that I did not understand in the place of translated English.

I bit my bottom lip, remembering how pissed the overseer was when I tried to explain that my translator was broken. The big, bald, horned fucker got angry with me, of course. He yelled at me and went bonkers with the use of the pain stick. I ended up biting my lip from the sheer pain and became so incensed by his brutality that I spat blood at him before he hurried off as though I had contaminated him.

Good. Next time, I'll throw up on him like a fucking vulture if it will keep him off me.

As I caught my breath, the door opened again, and I saw two males come in, the panel sliding closed behind them. "Oh great, what's this shit now?" I grumbled. Maybe I was lucky and Baldy had sent a tech for the translator.

I peered at the mismatched pair. One of them I had seen before—a smarmy little weasel who sometimes accompanied Baldy to look us over. Disgusted, I quickly shifted my gaze to his companion—and had to fight to keep my jaw from dropping.

Holy shit.

He didn't have horns and was bigger than any of the Omers I had seen. Though the strange alien had four arms and double pectorals like most Omers, he was taller, more muscular, and had a dangerous, wild, and untamed vibe. My body flushed as I imagined him as a shirtless warrior with sweat glistening on his hard body while he wielded a sword, slaying everyone who'd treated me like shit... starting with Baldy.

Against my better judgment, I was intrigued. Maybe it was the way he moved—with grace and lightness, despite his size. His weird haircut framed a face with full, sensual lips, a straight nose, and a square jaw that made my heart skip a beat. His sleeveless tunic and cloak with gold piping matched his eyes and were a nice touch. This alien was attractive.

I swallowed hard and quickly averted my eyes, knowing he'd caught me staring. *Busted.*

My head snapped up when I heard a sound. His lips were moving, but I couldn't understand a damn word he was saying because my translator was still malfunctioning. His eyes compelled me. They were a dark, intense yellow with flecks of gold that shimmered slightly as the light caught them.

Our gazes met, and I felt as if something silent was communicated between us.

Ella, this so not the time to think about sex.

I licked my lips before bringing the bottom one between my teeth. His nose twitched, and it sounded like he groaned. He took an enormous gulp as if he were nervous. His unease took some of the intimidation out of his menacing demeanor. My lips curled up into a smile. Then I caught myself.

Oh God. I'm flirting with a four-armed alien that might be here to buy me as his sex slave.

I tore my eyes away, recalling all the reasons I couldn't allow myself to fantasize about his hard, full lips, exotic, sexy eyes, or what was sure to be an impressive shredded set of abs beneath his clothes. Yet even as I tried to squash my surging desire, I felt my body respond, nipples going hard and cunt becoming wet with arousal.

What the fuck, Ella? Stop thinking impure thoughts. He's an alien that wants to sexually violate you.

I squeezed my hands between my knees and forced my lips into a frown.

The huge sexy being sniffed audibly before the two aliens communicated in their weird language. Now and again, my translator would cut back in and I would catch a few words before it quit again.

Earth... New... Untrained... Others?

The big, sexy-looking alien shook his head and folded both sets of arms, lifting his chin insistently. My translator buzzed, and then I heard him say, "No. This one tonight."

Did he just say he wants me?

They argued incomprehensibly for several more seconds, while all I could do was look for patterns in their speech and pick up every other word while watching their body language. The little one was gesturing around at the other cages and pointed at the door.

The big one simply shook his head again.

"No!" he said suddenly, quite clearly and so firmly that I stared at him again. "No one else will do."

My annoying translator cut out again. And I watched his sexy alien lips move.

What the hell is he talking about?

The smaller one nodded, plucking at the many jeweled rings on his fingers. He pulled out a dark-purple wand and touched it to my cage. I heard an audible beep, but the door did not open. The two spoke a little longer, none of it translating. Then they both turned and walked out.

Shit. I need to get someone to change the battery in this piece of crap translator so I can at least know what's going on.

I looked over at Sheryl napping in a ball

in her cage. "Yo, hey, Sheryl! Did they drug you?"

"Uh... no. I wish." She opened an eye and peered at me. "What's the deal?"

"My translator has stopped working. I think those little gray guys put the wrong battery in it or something. I need you to tell the damn overseer that it's crapped out on me." I crouched on the low, narrow seat, squirming as my ample ass overflowed it.

"Oh. Shit. Well, that's something they might fix. So you can't understand anything they're saying anymore?" She got up and stretched as best she could in her small cage, then jumped up and grabbed the bars, using them for pull-ups.

"I can hear every other word... sometimes more when this shit of a translator wants to work right. But in a nutshell, that little weasel-looking alien with all the rings was here with some giant, hot alien I've never seen before. They were talking about me. I think weasel was selling me, but I can't be sure." I was worried about that. I didn't like being kept in the dark about these damn aliens' plans for me.

Sheryl whistled. "Okay, don't sweat it. As soon as Baldy gets back, I'll let him know about your translator." She rubbed her eyes. "I just wish I'd been conscious for that mess... Maybe they are drugging me."

Or maybe we were both just short on sleep. This place was not at all kind to us in that respect. Sometimes we'd be able to grab a few hours of rest here and there, either lightly from anxiety or like a stone from exhaustion. But our accommodations were not exactly five star, and being balled up at the bottoms of our cages like some damn kittens was uncomfortable as hell. And to add to the indignity, we were expected to smile for potential buyers, be charming and demurely sexy—while we were constantly disoriented, hungry, cold, tired, and stiff from being caged like zoo animals.

Glancing around, I watched some of the women, who looked like they had cracked altogether, rocking back and forth. Frankly, I could see why many women probably picked being conditioned by the aliens as opposed to resistance. Their treatment of us was brutal, and insanity could easily slip into your mind before you knew it was happening. Maybe it was Stockholm syndrome or just the simple acceptance of circumstances. I didn't know, but I was going to fight—mentally and physically—to the bitter end.

"Thank you, Sheryl," I said very sincerely.

I didn't know what was going to happen next, but if I had to live without even knowing what my captors were saying to and about me, I might be the one ending up balled up and rocking on the floor of my cage.

CHAPTER 9

TEKEN

MY BODY WAS HUMMING, electrified by adrenaline as I paced restlessly in my room with Brax at my heels. I'd nearly gone berserk and shifted into my Wulfaen. I'd been consumed with the need to rip the cage open and claim what I instinctually recognized as mine.

She'd smelled so good, female and musky, frightened yet aroused... My burgeoning erection arose at the memory.

She's my one true mate. My sheleki. I'm certain of it. The gloriously beautiful female with long black hair, dark eyes, plush lips, skin the color of tree bark... and human.

So the Omers were correct—the earthlings

are compatible with my race. But how can I be bonded to a female from another race?

The notion of having a sheleki that was not a descendant of a Wulfaen Gladiator was unheard of among our people. But as soon as I smelled her alluring scent and locked eyes with her, I knew she was mine. My beast had growled in contentment, brushing against the inside of my skin. He started fighting to break free and make his own unique mark of claim on our earthling. I'd heard many stories of what it was like for Gladiators who finally found their mate—the animal urge to claim and mate nearly sending them crazy. Now I'd experienced the raw, primal hunger. I understood how it called to both forms in a way that defied anything I'd ever experienced.

And those despicable slavers had my female locked inside a cage like an animal. A dark-red haze of fury slid over my vision. Never had I experienced such a murderous rage. I didn't want to hurt, disarm, and disable. I needed to attack, demolish, and destroy —and my Wulfaen approved.

But I had to get my mood under control. I'd come here to do a job—one that would eventually lead to all of the females being freed. But now that I'd found my mate, she took priority over the initial mission.

I must free her. She is suffering, enraged, and must be loosed from her shackles and taken from this place.

I could not only see her frustration and fear, but I sensed her inner turmoil, which twisted up my guts with emotions.

I must get her out of here tonight!

My grandfather had instilled in me the value of intuition. Logic was a powerful force, but some things could not be reasoned. They could only be felt.

And right now, I had to get my female out of the slavers' grip—and I had to do it without blowing my cover. But I had to prepare the elders for my drastic change of plans. I was still obliged to complete my mission, but I refused to leave without her. I had the credits to buy her freedom, but I didn't want the slavers who held her captive to profit from setting her free.

Storming over to the wall of windows that overlooked the luxuriantly planted courtyard, I pushed open the huge middle section. The jungle scents washed my nostrils, cleaning the aromas of perfume, sweat, and old wine that permeated this horrible place. Pulling a folded messenger drone from my belt—because I couldn't afford anyone picking up my broadcast—I pressed the tip of the little capsule, which glowed yellow, and spoke in a low tone.

"I must leave at once," I insisted. "I will explain when I get back to the pack. I will be bringing my ma—" I cut off the word. I did not want to raise expectations among the elders or pack that the earthlings were the solution to our race's mating problem when finding my mate among them could just be an anomaly.

"I will be bringing one of the informants that we need with me. Someone will need to come and take my place here, and you can expect higher security due to my disappearance. I will explain upon my return."

I released the drone into the air.

I hated having to abandon my mission, but the pounding, desperate urgency to free my mate would not leave my head. My job was to obey the visceral need to protect her while making sure she knew she could trust me.

I needed private access to her to communicate that I intended to get her out of this place. But the only way to do that and not arouse suspicion had been to order her sent to my room for my night's "entertainment." Yet another stomach-turning practice of this place —and apparently, she would be drugged as well. Fortunately, I had ways of dealing with that.

I just hoped I could keep from making a fool of myself if she was delivered stuffed full of aphrodisiacs, but I pushed aside the thought. I was a man of honor, and I would do nothing to take advantage of her.

Brax sensed me relaxing slightly and sat beside me, his tail thudding against my hip. I scratched his ears. "Well, old friend, there's been a change of plans. I know you probably would like to sleep in that fine bed all night, but we've got some traveling to do."

The genetically engineered creature cocked his head at me, then rolled over, demanding belly scratches. Of all the alien base species we had taken for modification, Earth dogs were one of the absolute best. Especially when they were big enough to carry two people over crazy terrain, fight off monsters, and hunt their own meat. I knew the creature that had emerged from our labs was very large by Earth standards and had some other modifications, but I hoped Brax's presence would help calm the female.

Hopefully, she would not be so broken down by her experiences thus far that I would be unable to reach her with a reasoned explanation. If I could just talk to her for a few minutes, I was certain I could gain her trust enough to facilitate our escape.

All I needed right now was a stroke of luck.

CHAPTER 10

ELLA

IT TURNED out Sheryl never had the chance to talk to the overseer before two attendants came in and started rolling my cage out of the room.

"Wait!" she yelled, but they ignored her.

I shot her a helpless look before disappearing out of sight.

I was worried. The farthest I'd been out of the room was to the bathroom. Now they were wheeling me down a long hallway lined with what looked like advertising panels. Then it dawned on me that the panels were meant to acclimate the aliens' captives—like me—to the foreign world they were now in. But after weeks of constant exposure to their "commercials," I hated the sight of them. I would give anything for a dark, quiet room where I could just curl up on a real bed and sleep for days. Instead, I was struggling to keep my wits about me as the aliens finally stopped before one of the silver door panels and opened it.

My cage was shoved inside, and one of the attendants stayed behind, turning on a set of blessedly dim lights. He rounded on me, his pale-yellow eyes glowing slightly in the dimness. I realized he had reflections at the backs of his eyes, as a cat would. He inched forward and opened the cage door, gesturing for me to step out.

I nodded and obeyed. Trying to run and escape was futile.

The few times I'd tried, I'd ended up running through what felt like a maze of hallways with no exit. And the aliens always caught me easily and then punished me severely for attempting to escape. I learned the hard way that the layout of this alien prison was disorientating and there was no way out without help from the inside.

I scanned the space, which wasn't very large. But it had a computer array of some sort covering one wall, a cushy-looking beige suede couch lining the wall across from it, and one of their toilet-shower pod things set into the back wall.

He ran a scanner over me, and the screen behind him started lighting up with more of those golden symbols. He frowned and nodded and then looked up and spoke to me unintelligibly. When I didn't respond, he scowled and repeated himself in a sharper tone.

At the end of my rope, I shook my head, pointed to my ear, and said in what I presumed was completely untranslated English, "I have no idea what you are saying. This piece of shit translator of yours is broken."

He paused, brow furrowing, then peered at me and asked a question in a mildly shocked but much calmer tone. I shook my head and then tried to take off one of the damned earrings so I could show him. He saw what I was doing and nodded, reaching for a pair of the funky-looking tongs the little gray alien had used to initially set the gold disks in my ears.

I held still as he removed the right one with a click, took it in hand, and winced. The crystal set into the back was completely black, and the gold contacts connected to it had become discolored. I was surprised it hadn't zapped me or burned my ear.

He rumbled something that was probably a description of how fucked up my translator was and then looked back at me, nodding. He removed the other earring and tossed both into a drawer, then gestured me toward the shower pod.

Usually, they barely let me rinse off the damn lather before they kicked me out and shoved me into another exotic lingerie set. This time, though, the alien let me scrub off for a long time as he spoke into a small silvery communicator wand. I hoped at least I would be able to overhear my captors again soon.

I washed my hair and scoured my body, letting the hot spray loosen my stiff muscles. Afterward, I stood in the steam, working oil through my thick hair and finger-combing it. When I emerged, I felt a hell of a lot better, even if I was still apprehensive about whatever was going on.

The clothes I had stripped off were gone when I stepped out of the pod. He had left me a bundle of garments on the couch, along with a pair of gold suede ballet slipper shoes and a bottle of shimmering gold cream. I eagerly rubbed the cream all over my skin, glad to finally treat the dry, rough patches on my knees and elbows.

The cream had a scent this time—sweet, rich, slightly musky. I smiled a little as I rubbed it in, checking my look in the mirror beside the bathroom pod. It made my skin shimmer like someone had sprinkled me with gold dust. I pulled on the breast harness and another of those loincloths, which I hastily tied around my hips and crotch. I was getting a little tired of feeling everything I sat on against my bare snatch.

The gown I was to wear over it was so fine it was almost transparent and so soft I almost wanted to wear it without underwear. But I had never been one for the naked-in-a-clear-raincoat look, so I kept the harness and my other clothes on. I was just stepping into the shoes when the attendant returned, carrying what looked like a large toolbox.

It turned out to be a makeup case, and he sat me down on the couch and turned on some bright lights around me before bending over me with the brush. More of that gold stuff went on my eyelids. He painted my lips a slightly darker shade of red-brown and then glazed it to give my lips a wet look. My eyelashes and brows didn't need any help.

He worked quickly, his hands moving nimbly at different tasks, dizzying me a little. Soon enough, my hair was braided and coiled, my face primped, my nails shaped and painted in gold, and my body perfumed. As a crowning touch, he reached for a small spray vial, this one clear and filled with a thick-looking deep-red liquid. He raised it and then unexpectedly sprayed me in the face with it.

I blinked my eyes closed too late and felt an odd tingle in my tear ducts. *Is that sealer? I really hope it's hypoallergenic.*

He nodded once, then gestured to the couch and wheeled my cage out, leaving me alone. I heard the door lock behind him, and I sighed, settling on the brown suede cushions and stretching out. I didn't know if my chance to rest was a matter of kindness or a prelude to something more sinister, but I stretched luxuriantly and then rolled over on my belly, pillowing my cheek on my arms.

I didn't know how long I lay there dozing when I became aware of a warm flush running through my body. It started around my eyes and mouth and stretched outward slowly, relaxing me as it spread. It felt like something impossibly soft brushing against my skin. And then... it began to intensify.

I rolled over, staring up at the ceiling. It felt a little like a pot high but more acute and sensual. I squeezed my legs together and moaned softly. My mind and body were at war. My body craved the touch of a man, but my mind was trying to shut down my wanton need.

What's happening?

Then I remembered the red fluid that fucker sprayed me with.

He drugged me!

The realization made me want to fight the sexual need that was wrapping around me like a vine, but my primal need was too intense and far too pleasant. And it was still growing.

I need to be fucked—fast and hard—now.

Within minutes, I was writhing and trembling on the couch, my breath coming in whimpers. Every sensation had turned into pleasure.

I rubbed myself against the couch, wondering if I could get off just from that. But even when I started caressing my own body, I couldn't orgasm. I was stuck creeping toward the edge of sexual nirvana but unable to push myself over on my own.

I was starting to get desperate when the attendant returned, looking a hell of a lot hotter than he had before the drug. I struggled to keep myself from holding out my arms to him, and it took all I had to resist begging the alien to fuck me senseless.

He nodded, apparently satisfied by the state the drug had left me in, and gave me a spray from another vial full of crystal-blue fluid. I immediately became very drowsy, and he helped me to my feet, leading me out and down the hall.

The feel of my thighs rubbing together and my nipples brushing against the harness kept me at a full boil as we went downstairs in a transparent elevator. I watched in a dream-like state as we stood inside the clear shaft that glided past three floors full of slave trainees.

Finally, we reached the right floor and stepped out, turning down another of those ad-filled hallways. My heart was pounding and I desperately wanted to start rubbing myself, but I forced my hands to stay at my sides. I wasn't going to masturbate in front of this asshole alien.

The attendant stepped forward and knocked on the door. After a few moments, it slid open. Framed in the doorway was Mr. Alien Hottie, gazing down at us with a smile on his face. His eyes fixed on me, and after a moment, the attendant stepped back and I threw myself into the big alien's four arms.

CHAPTER 11

TEKEN

THE DOOR CLOSED on the attendant's smirk as my mate rubbed her soft body against me, panting and trembling with need. My body responded at once, my lower arms wrapping around her and my cock swelling with the strong urge to claim her.

I buried my face in her hair, completely swept up in the moment as she offered herself to me. For long, agonizing heartbeats, I couldn't force myself nor my inner beast to pull away from her. She was our female.

She writhed against me, and the power of that blatant invitation made my head swim. I wanted to kiss her—even though I knew that the moment I did, neither of us would be in control. *And then I'll have to live with myself. No. I will not do that to her.*

If I kissed her, it would start the mating process with the exchange of pheromones. After that, our bodies and emotions would start to synchronize, and the need to mate would begin to overcome not just the drive to complete my mission—getting her back to my pack alive—but even my survival instinct. Properly bonded Gladiators didn't emerge from their mating bower for days after their first kiss.

My lips still hovered near hers. Disastrously near. My incisors lengthened, ready to nip her bottom lip playfully.

She's so tempting... Just one lick and—

No! I must not.

I groaned aloud from the feel of my aching cock, dizziness in my head, and a terrible hunger to be touched. This female was driving me toward a mating frenzy.

Logic finally took hold.

She's drugged. This is not her will.

Quickly, I backed off, holding her gently at arm's length.

Her moan was deep and throaty.

It took every ounce of my self-control to hold her away from me and reach for the counter-intoxicant on my belt. I couldn't risk her hating me—or me despising myself—so I pulled the spray from its pocket and puffed a good dose into her face.

She gasped in surprise, pulling the vapors into her lungs, then coughed. I held her steady, not embracing her, just supporting her as she got a bit wobbly. I sighed with relief. The drug was wearing off.

I refuse to let my first time with the sheleki the gods chose for me be marred by intoxicants given to her against her will. It would taint everything we'd potentially have, and this I cannot allow. There was nothing more important on this planet to me than her—my mate— and there never would be. Not our children. Not my pack. Only my sheleki.

Her dilated dark eyes slowly returned to normal, pupils contracting, and her breathing calmed. Once she seemed steady on her feet again, I gently let her go.

"Are you all right?" I asked.

She blinked at me blankly and then looked down at herself, shuddering. Realization broke over her face, and the hazy look of confusion turned into a mix of fear, outrage, and—when she glanced at me—relief. At least she understood that I was not behind her drugging and had refused to take advantage of her.

It hurt to pull away from her, especially when I could still smell her arousal, a fine perfume of feminine musk that wafted inside my nostrils, making it impossible for my body to settle down. I endured, keeping my distance even as she stared at me in the most alluring way.

"I am sorry." I started. "None of this was my doing. Please understand that I mean you no harm." I spread my hands in a pacifying gesture. "I am a Wulfaen Gladiator, and our oath is to honor and protect our females."

She shook her head, pointing at her ears.

It was then that I noticed something was different. She opened her mouth and started talking, and I knew something was very wrong.

Why can't I understand her?

What came out of her mouth was a confusing jumble of noises. It was a language, mostly in midrange tones, with a wide range of sounds and an inflection that clearly conveyed her confusion and anger.

I frowned, pointing at my ear. "Can you understand me?"

The two-armed female furrowed her brow, looking me up and down. She glanced to the spray in my hand and seemed to understand that I had cured her fabricated arousal, even if the slightest bit of affection from her had left me fervently wishing it wasn't artificial. She relaxed slightly, though her distress was clear on her pretty face.

Slowly, she reached up and gestured at her ears. Her translator buds were missing, though her ears had clearly been pierced.

I blinked and gestured at my own ear again.

She sighed, and the frustration showed just as clearly as the disquiet had.

She has no translator. Curse it! This will make it much more difficult to explain my plan to her.

Her stare panned the room, and it appeared it was the first time she noticed Brax. She squeaked, her eyes widening.

Brax rolled over and sat up, thudding his tail against the bed. She swallowed and moved forward a little. I followed, ready to muffle any screams in case my dog got too playful. The only problem with riding dogs was when they decided it was playtime, they could wreck a whole room and cover you in slobber before getting their senses back, especially younger ones like Brax.

I moved forward to make certain things did not get out of hand. Maybe because Brax's species was from Earth, my human was drawn to him. It could be comforting to see something familiar, even if the animal was probably ten times the normal size of an Earth dog.

Brax scooted toward her on the bed, his tail bashing against the liquid gel mattress so hard that it rippled. She proved brave, taking another step forward while glancing at me uncertainly. Then Brax lost his patience and lunged forward, leading with his tongue. With one enormous slurp, he removed most of her makeup and several crystals off her outfit while applying a liberal coating of doggy drool.

"Brax!" I yelled. Then I looked at her and saw her standing there wide-eyed and dripping, frozen in a hunched-shoulder pose, while Brax wagged his tail and play bowed.

I clapped three hands over my face. *I should never have brought a near puppy on a mission like this.*

I moved toward her, trying to figure out how to apologize profusely using only gestures, when I heard an unexpected sound. She laughed. The sound caught me off guard, and it intensified until she was half doubled over. She braced her palms on those lush thighs, and tears gathered at the corners of her eyes as she had what was probably her first good laugh in months. Finally, she sat on the edge of the bed.

I grabbed Brax's harness and held him back from slobbering her again as she struggled to pull herself together. I fished out the cleaning towel and handed it to her. She continued tittering as she started absently mopping her face and hair with it. She didn't seem to notice the little silvery trails of nanites cleansing her skin and hair before retreating to the patch of cloth.

She gave me a weak little smile and nod of thanks as she caught her breath, and then the laughing started up again. I had thought it was good humor, but I didn't know much about human women. I paid closer attention and sat down nearby, just observing her.

When she started talking, I didn't stop her or gesture my lack of comprehension. She rambled on, gesturing, tears filling her eyes as I realized she was too overwrought for even Brax's ridiculous self to fix it for long.

It was like watching a jump ship's heat stack vent after a journey, the meaning of her words less important than her using them as an outlet for what couldn't stay inside.

So I sat and listened as her words got faster and jumbled together and finally turned into sobs. Brax whined and laid his broad muzzle on her thigh, eyebrows wiggling in canine worry. I laid a few hands on her shoulders and back.

She wept, and I struggled to comfort her. I suddenly understood a little how Brax felt. Without the tool of words, I was limited in my ability to reassure her. At least she didn't seem offended when I touched her.

I knew beyond the shadow of a doubt that I had done the right thing by not kissing her earlier. I had absolutely no interest in a union that involved any form of slavery. Either we mutually agreed we belonged to each other or there was no future for us as mates.

When she had recovered enough, she looked up at me with a teary smile and again didn't seem to notice when the nanites stole the tears off her cheeks. She started scratching Brax's ears absently, and he began thudding his tail again.

The female and I locked eyes.

She hesitated, then laid her hand against her chest and said one of those unfamiliar words and repeated it. "Ella."

Is that her name? I repeated it, pointing at her. "El-la?"

She nodded, looking slightly relieved.

I put a hand on my chest as she had done. "Teken."

Her brows drew together. "Te-ken."

I nodded and smiled, then gave her a serious look and pointed toward the wall of windows. *Outside.* I didn't know how to communicate with her my desire that we escape—and as soon as possible—but I had to try.

She followed my gesture and then stood and moved over to the large opening in the wall that displayed the great forest spread out to the horizon, and I heard her gasp.

Moving away from the bed, I walked toward her, Brax trailing behind me. I hoped she understood my intentions to break her out of this disgusting place.

CHAPTER 12

ELLA

I STARED through the panel of windows at the alien landscape. My head was spinning as I struggled to process everything that was happening. Even with my malfunctioning translator, I recognized the word "Wulfaen." He was from the race of Gladiators the Omers were trying to sell us humans to. Which meant he wanted me for sex.

I frowned. *But if that's true, why didn't he try to take advantage of me when I was high on the arousal drug?* Without much effort, he could have taken me in every position possible.

Instead of dominating me when he clearly had the upper hand, he showed restraint and respect—and his actions went a long way with me.

Maybe my luck had changed and I'd run into the only alien in this damn place with any real sense of morality and decency. He'd held all the cards when I was brought to his room, and he didn't have to administer the antidote to the aphrodisiac from hell. But he did, even though a boner the size of Florida was pressed against my belly.

His behavior so far spoke well of his integrity and made me more interested in knowing more about him, especially if he was willing to help me leave this alien prison.

Then there was his incredibly affectionate alien dog, who had an adult body and a mild case of puppy personality. Frankly, I was a sucker for animals. But most importantly, both alien and dog had treated me well and seemed genuinely concerned about me when I had broken down into ugly tears.

Teken, unlike his fellow alien bruisers, seemed downright chivalrous—so far. Maybe he was a cut above his peers, or maybe he was married. Though, the way he had held me tenderly—and his gigantic erection while doing it—said he had been tempted by me but backed off, showing restraint.

Teken strode over to the left of me.

Damn... he smells nice. Kind of spicy with an undertone of pine trees and earth.

For a moment, I wondered what it would feel like to have his two sets of hands caressing my skin. I shook my head, worried a little that I was still drugged, because it was seriously crazy to be thinking about this strange but oddly sexy creature in such a sensual way.

That's what I get for staying celibate for so long. Now I was thinking about putting Teken on my "to-be-fucked" list.

His dog pressed his huge body along my right side as if trying to comfort me. I petted him slowly, mesmerized by the shaggy, heavily muscled black creature with too many teeth. But under that menacing veneer, he was a sweet puppy dog. I just wished his one good lick hadn't undone my entire shower and most of my makeup. At least the weird silvery cloth Teken had handed me cleaned me off quickly.

Teken pointed again to the landscape and said something in that oddly inflected alien tongue. My best guess was he was asking me if I wanted to leave with him.

I just stared through the window at the unusual scenery. The sight of the alien terrain terrified me, strange and beautiful as it was.

I pushed down my fears.

I'd rather be free on this planet than drugged, caged, and waiting to be conditioned. And if Teken was willing to help me escape, then I was going to take a chance and trust him. Frankly, I had nothing to lose at this point. At least outside, I had a fighting chance of survival, as opposed to inside this alien abode of doom.

I nodded at Teken, but I wished I had the means to communicate to him that my agreement was conditional. I didn't want to leave Sheryl or any of the other females caged up like animals. I didn't care if they were human or alien; we were all the same—victims of slave trafficking—and no woman deserved to go through that shit. But I knew that what I wanted might not be possible or the smartest thing to attempt when I was so close to attaining my freedom.

But how can I just run and leave them behind?

Guilt made my stomach churn. Now emotionally and mentally torn, I stared at him.

Fuck! I would kill for a translator right about now so I could make him understand this place was crowded with so many captives. Not that I wasn't grateful, but... *Why did he choose me over one of them?*

I tapped his shoulder—his muscle felt like polished wood under silk—and gestured at my ear and throat. He frowned for a moment, then sighed and nodded, saying something I couldn't understand. This time, he gave me an apologetic look as he pointed back at the windows.

I frowned. I was trying not to get frustrated, but he didn't make it very easy. Then something important dawned on me.

Right now, the slavers expected us to spend at least the next hour fucking. This was the only time they knew where I was but didn't have any eyes on me and the only time he could act outside their view as well. Plus, they would expect us to be... occupied—not taking off.

"Damn, you're hot *and* smart," I commented with a sigh of relief.

Fine. I'll go with him, get a translator, see what help I can get, and then come back to free the others. There's no way I'm letting Sheryl end up a drugged, brainwashed fucktoy.

But I needed something to wear that wasn't alien fetish gear. Otherwise, I was going to freeze my tits off out there in the elements. Turning to glance around the room, I spotted the huge, worn chestnut-colored pouches that looked like saddlebags nestled at the side of one of the mammoth beds. From the expanded nature of the bags, I could tell they were packed with a lot of stuff. Maybe this was his luggage and he had something inside that I could wear.

I pointed over to the bags and said, "Do you have something I can change into?"

His face wrinkled with confusion.

Okay. This communication issue is going to be a pain in the ass.

Not wasting any more time, I strode over to the saddlebags, reaching down to pick them up, but they were crazy heavy. Teken walked over to me, then said something in a grumbly but kind tone as he gently removed my hands from the bags, hoisting them easily onto the bed.

He uttered something and looked at me questioningly.

I ran my hands down my body illustratively. "Clothes."

His gaze panned down to my cleavage and lingered there. He looked so flustered; I wondered if this was the first time he'd been around a human female.

He said something, then took off his teal and gold tunic and handed it over.

With my arms full of thick, silky cloth, I stared at him. The flexible gray armor he wore underneath was even more formfitting. Every part of him was as ripped as his arms: broad chest with double pectorals, massive shoulders, clipped waist, and powerful thighs. The bulge of his codpiece made me wonder if my slow perusal turned him on.

Eyes off the alien's cock, Ella. Focus. Escape. Freedom. Now.

I finally managed to tear my stare away from his amazing body and fumble my way into his tunic. The sleek fabric slid over my body in a long, warm caress as I tugged my head through the collar and settled the fabric over my breasts. The tunic was cut to allow two sets of burly arms through each armhole, which meant only the leather harness beneath prevented me from showing massive side boob. I could live with that. But that left a bit of a problem. The tunic, which reached his knees, drooped to the floor on me. I looked like a little girl playing dress-up.

I could make a whole nightgown out of one of his T-shirts. And I'm not a small lady.

I frowned, staring down at myself, and heard him fight back a laugh. I glanced up. He was pinching the bridge of his nose and looking away while his shoulders shook a little.

"Oh yeah, very funny," I groused at him, and my tone must have set him off because he burst out snickering... and I joined him.

Dammit, I've been in hell for weeks. How is it that his mere presence can make me feel so much better so fast?

My laughter faded away when I realized this alien had done something no Earth man or alien had ever managed to do—make me lower my emotional guard.

Fuck! I'm going to have to watch it around Teken. There's no way I'm getting emotionally involved with him, not when I'm heading back home.

Quickly, I peered around for something that might serve to belt up the enormous thing so I could at least walk in it. I finally settled on a thick gold rope, which held the room's decorative wreath together, yanking it down and tying it around my waist, then using that to tuck up the bottom artfully. It didn't even look half bad in the mirror now—and I could travel by night without freezing to death.

Turning, I nodded to him, folding my arms, and I saw him dragging what looked like horse tack out from under the bed. I stepped back, watching as he called the dog over and started buckling the heavy, padded leather straps around him. Then he fastened a broad saddle that was more cushion and grips across the dog's back and finished by attaching the chestnut-colored pouches securely to the saddle using ties.

I looked from him to the dog and was a little shocked when he swung one powerfully muscled leg over the animal and jumped into the saddle. He looked at me, scooted back some, and patted the space between the dog's neck and him.

I hesitated, glancing back at the door. *Sorry, Sheryl. I'll be back for you. I promise.*

Stepping forward, I grabbed Teken's proffered hand and slipped onto the saddle in front of him.

His lower arms wrapped around me. Then he bent forward, all but pressing me into the furry neck, while his upper arms firmly clutched the dog's barrel chest.

He shouted what sounded like a command. I didn't understand why he'd taken so much care to steady and cover me until the dog bolted forward, straight toward the wall of open windows. He was so big that he burst the panels from their frames with a bang. Now we were outside, plummeting, and although I knew it was more of a jump for the dog and I should be safe, I was shaking like a leaf and screamed the whole way down.

CHAPTER 13

TEKEN

ELLA GAVE A LOUD, piercing cry as we made the leap. I hung on to her, curling my body around her to ensure she was safe and would not fall off Brax.

Effortlessly, my dog bounded out of the window, heading downward gracefully until we met the ground with a soft bounce. Then with another bounce, he cleared the tree line, landing with a thump in the bushes. Behind us, the complex alarms shrilled.

After guiding Brax to the small copse of trees, I hopped off his back, storming over to yank my hidden gear bag from under the soil. Panting, Ella gave a wide-eyed glance over her shoulder, taking in the height of the opening we'd just flown through, gulping as her eyes traced down to the ground. She appeared stunned and maybe a bit terrified, but she had nothing to worry about; our safety was Brax's top priority.

After stowing my gear in the pouches attached to the saddle, I jumped back on and patted Brax's shoulder. "Good dog. Take us home."

I held Ella very carefully as we rode, knowing we had to get as much distance between us and the slavers before we stopped again, but I was concerned that she was likely unaccustomed to riding. I had no idea what her life was like on Earth, but I had a growing notion that Ella was not familiar with roughing it. She seemed refined and inexperienced in physical risk, though brave in the face of terrible hardship.

I had a good sense of others, and she seemed kind and smart. Obviously, she was ravishing. My mind raced back to the exorbitant price the slavers had demanded for private time with her, even though they stressed Ella was untrained. Since she was my mate, price was no object to me, and I would do anything to protect her and keep her by my side.

I inhaled deeply until my chest burned. *My mate smells so good.* It was the kind of fragrance a Gladiator could lose himself in—clean, fresh, tantalizing, arousing, and... female.

My cock swelled and pulsed as I imagined peeling off her clothes and running my tongue along her soft skin before my head disappeared between her strong legs to devour her sweet nectar.

I would part her seam, lick from bottom to top, tease her, and lap her up until she screamed my name over and over again.

She would taste incredible. I was certain of it.

My cock was aching and my heavy balls armed and ready to pump my seed into my mate's womb to seal the bond between us while marking her with my bite that would show all males that she was mine to protect and cherish. My Wulfaen pressed against my skin, anxious for me to start the mating process, officially claiming her. But marking Ella would involve her implicit trust and consent.

Then there was the fact that I had no idea how to sexually please a human. All of my knowledge attained from the simulator assumed that my mate would be a female of our race. Ella was not strong or resilient like female Gladiators of the past who enjoyed rutting nonstop until her mate's seed planted a pup. Humans were too weak to take what a Gladiator required—hard and fast fucking.

I shook my head in an attempt to cool the powerful arousal coursing through my body like molten fire.

I had to proceed slowly with Ella. She was an earthling, and my sexual urges and desires would probably be very confusing to her, even with the aid of translators. Plus, after everything she'd most likely been through at the hands of the slavers, it would be unfair of me to expect that she'd readily respond to the mating bond between us.

Patience would be needed to win both her trust and heart, especially now that we were fleeing for our lives.

My mouth tightened. Things had not gone as planned at the slavers' facility, which would result in lots of tension between the council and me once I'd revealed what I'd done—freed my mate and stolen what the Omers viewed as property.

It bothered me that if the Omers ever found out that it was a Gladiator who stole Ella, they would view the act cause for war with my people. Not that the Omers were a match against the Gladiators—they were not—but it made me uneasy that my actions could possibly put our packs in danger.

On a positive note, I'd gained a lot of information about the facility and its practices, and once Ella had a functioning translator, she would be able to give us more details about her captivity and how many females still awaited rescuing.

My mouth tightened just thinking about the females the slavers continued to hold in captivity.

On my honor, I will return with my pack and rescue them.

Brax chuffed loudly. The sound meant he was happy to be out running again after being penned up in my suite. He bounded over boulders and fallen trees, eager for home. And finally, Ella's body relaxed enough to enjoy the ride. I clung to her carefully as the fast, jostling trip took us safely through the deep brush.

As we went, I spoke to her, even knowing it was pointless. She was my mate, and silence felt strange. According to what I knew about humans, they were often chatty, filling up space with words even if there wasn't anything to talk about. I supposed in the absence of a strong pheromone response, they needed to feel connected somehow—just as Brax needed physical contact, affection, companionship, and play to strengthen the connection between us.

"We must continue on, for which I am sorry," I said as Brax scrambled up a sloped rock outcrop. "I would give you more of a chance to get used to everything that is happening, but I cannot."

Ella, so far, had made no sounds of complaint after that initial shocked scream when we'd jumped through the window. Now she just hung on to Brax's scruff, and every so often, she'd talk. But of course, I couldn't understand what she was saying. Her language sounded a little like the chirping of birds, though musical and with a lot less screeching. I focused on the different words, determined to learn a bit the hard way in case we were delayed in our journey overland.

Anything could happen at this point due to the fact that we were now on the run. I knew the slavers would send their best catchers after us. They usually used hover vehicles instead of dogs, which was tactically foolish since the loud vibrations from their hoverpads drew hordes of local predators. To compensate for the noisy commotion they were known to create, the slave catchers tended to speed through the air, which meant they would probably overshoot and miss us entirely in the dark.

"When they come for us, we will let them circle around until they draw out the beasts of the woods, who will drive them back home," I mused aloud.

She turned her head slightly and tilted it up to meet my gaze, her curiosity making me smile again.

"Eventually, when they are off our trail, we will return to my pack."

She spoke, then patted one of my arms, ending her words with my name. I hoped she at least knew I would protect her with my last breath, and I resumed my mental assessment of our tactical evasion strategies.

The catchers can't scan for life when we're surrounded by greenery. In woods this thick, their bio scanners will give off-the-scale readings in every direction. Those foolish slavers developed all their tech on that desolate rock of theirs, and they don't know what to do with a forest.

I tightened my grip on Ella and Brax as he bounded over another enormous fallen tree. Something huge and camouflaged lunged at us from the side, but Brax simply left it in our dust as its unfurling tentacles briefly flickered into view.

We had been running for some time now, and in the deep green shadows of the forest, it was easy to relax and assume we were free from any risk aside from the creatures that lived here. But I knew better. I had killed a few slave catchers in my time, mostly when they had strayed into Gladiator territory, so I knew they were doggedly persistent.

At least I didn't have to worry about their knowing I was a Gladiator. The slavers had no idea yet I'd set into motion a plan to gather information about their facility to shut them down. But I had fouled up part of my mission. I still hoped the council and elders would understand when I explained my reason for changing my errand.

There isn't one among the Gladiators who doesn't long for the chance to have a mate of his own. Perhaps I am selfish, and if so, I will atone for my actions. But could any warrior among us have resisted?

I honestly don't think so.

But in retrospect, I had a bigger problem.

I'd found my mate at the slavers' facility. Once I got back to my pack and word spread to the other alphas that Ella was my one true mate, there would be contention among the packs to seize as many earthlings as possible for their Gladiators.

Will the frenzy to hoard the females provoke another war among the packs? Or will cooler heads prevail, and can we deal with the earthling issue in an orderly fashion—and without war?

"We will have to keep ahead of the catchers," I told Ella. "They are who the slavers will send after us." I was under no illusion that she understood me, but right now, it was enough that I communicated with her and reassured her with my touch and tone.

I wanted to tell her more... *That she is my mate and I will kill anyone who tries to hurt her.*

I wished to explain that her mere presence lifted my heart, and for once in my life, I felt there was hope for happiness in my future. But I knew she would not understand the way of the Gladiators or the loneliness that consumed all of us—including me.

I sighed heavily just thinking about the fact that the Gladiator life had not changed all that much since we'd won our freedom from the Omers. Gladiators still took a binding oath to maintain our risky way of life until our deaths and trained for bloody combat. But instead of fighting for coins to make the Omers wealthier, most Gladiators went on missions for hire—on our planet and others—earning top compensation. And others enjoyed staying close to their packs, safeguarding the general good of our race and the protection of our expanding territory.

Those that chose to remain within the pack spent their time training tirelessly, but there was more to life than just making your body a finely tuned combat vessel. We needed the softness of a female. A mate to keep our hearts and souls alive.

There was only so long a warrior could bear the emotional isolation of not having a female to share his life with, and this was sometimes difficult for even the most disciplined mind to stave off. Which was why Ella and I simply had to survive long enough for us to get home and celebrate with the pack that the gods had gifted me with my long-awaited mate.

My thoughts snapped to the present when I heard the faint whine of hover vehicles swelling in the distance behind us, and I knew getting us back safely was going to be a difficult prospect—at least for a while.

CHAPTER 14

ELLA

"I DON'T KNOW what the fuck you're saying, big guy, but I'm sure you know what you're doing." This was my go-to response whenever Teken rumbled at me again.

His speech had a liquid inflection and tended to run together a lot more than English. I was trying to sort out its patterns, but it was challenging. I hadn't expected an immersive crash course in alien linguistics to be part of my escape, but as problems went, a language barrier was a lot better to deal with than being locked up and waiting to be sold.

The ride through the woods on the back of a giant dog had taken some getting used to. The constant jostling left me sore and motion sick at first, but eventually, I got used to it enough that it just tired me out. The only thing that made the whole thing bearable was I was carefully held in Teken's arms.

He never made a sexually inappropriate move. Despite his having four hands to keep track of, somehow, none of them wandered. He impressed me, though his control frustrated me, too, because oddly, I was attracted to him. Remembering the aching heat of the moment when I'd thrown myself into his arms, I wished I could replay the whole scene without the drugs or the language barrier. Or the horrible slaver facility, for that matter.

But my captors were in the past—I hoped —and I did my best to adjust to my current situation as the dog bounded us over or around every obstacle we came across. Giant trees, upright or fallen—no damn problem. Streams, rivers, lakes—the big dog handled that shit in a single bound. Huge flesh-eating masses of tentacles lunging at us out of nowhere—*whoosh*... just outrun it.

I didn't understand why there was a dog here on this alien planet at all, let alone one that looked like a weaponized Newfoundland. I knew that parallel evolution was a thing and

Earth dogs didn't have shark teeth or the mass of an elephant. But everything about this creature's behavior screamed "dog," from its wagging tail to slobbery tongue to tremendous enthusiasm about everything.

It was strangely comforting that I was being safely whisked away. Just like the careful half embrace of the four-armed giant alien seated behind me. Of course, the dog didn't leave me slightly hot and bothered with my hormones at a slow burn for hours of hard riding. And my current feelings didn't have shit to do with the drug. I was sure of it now. It was him. He was a hulking stranger, but if I had thought he was hot when I'd first seen him from inside my cage, now that I understood he was a Wulfaen Gladiator with the desire to set me free instead of buying me as his sex slave, he was sizzling.

And then there was our conversation. We talked to each other without knowing the other's language, and sometimes, we managed to teach each other a word or two. I stumbled around the pronunciation of some words, while his accent gave a lyrical tone to everything he said. Mostly, we communicated by tone, body language, and gestures. And by the time I felt his big body tense behind me for the first time since our escape, we had sorted out a few words between us.

The dog's name was Brax. The word for "dog" seemed to be *iemnon*. I didn't know what the word *tagah* meant when he spat it out immediately after stiffening, but it sounded like a curse.

"What is it?" I asked, and he scowled and shook his head slightly.

He said something to Brax, who immediately turned to bound into even deeper brush, flushing out a small swarm of what looked like enormous fuzzy moths from the bushes. Startled, I hung on, nestling back against Teken and shielding my face as branches slapped against us from both sides.

A few moments later, I heard a faint whine rising above sounds of crashing and rustling. The noise came closer and closer, and a chill went down my spine. *Oh shit. That sounds like a vehicle.* And it was coming from the direction of the compound he had just broken me out of.

We kept running. To my surprise, the big alien did not urge more speed from his mount, but instead seemed determined to keep us heading through the thickest sections of brush and trees. It would have been easier to follow one of the streams, but for some reason, he wanted us as far as possible from open sky.

I realized why a few minutes later when the whine rose to ear-stinging levels and was accompanied by a whooshing. Lights appeared over our heads. Something was flying above the tree line, bringing a hot wind with it. Trees tossed. Leaves blew. And suddenly, Teken's choice of path made perfect sense. He shouted to Brax, and we slid to a stop in the depths of a thicket.

I struggled for breath as I clung to the dog, chest heaving in desperation for my next gulp of air. Brax was panting enthusiastically. But behind me, Teken sat silent, face tilted upward, watchful.

The group of—I didn't know if they were aircraft or not—whooshed overhead in a widely spaced formation. Searchlights and what looked like some odd sort of greenish laser strobe beamed out from their undersides, flicking over the trees and rock outcroppings, searching everywhere the light could penetrate.

The Omers were searching for us.

I held my breath as the light moved closer and closer, scanning back and forth in an overlapping pattern.

Don't find us. Don't find us.

I knew in my heart what sort of brutal shit would happen if they did. I wasn't just scared for myself. I didn't want Teken or Brax to pay for rescuing me. The big alien didn't seem to have any kind of weapon on him, aside from the small, odd-looking pistol at his belt, and I knew the hunters would be better armed.

I shivered violently, burying my head against Brax's fur, tears stinging my eyes.

I can't go back.

I hated feeling so helpless and scared.

Maybe if I had a gun in my hands and wasn't completely exhausted and overwhelmed, I would be able to push down my fears and get my act together. But right now, panic gripped me, and I couldn't risk running or even moving.

All four of Teken's arms encircled me, holding me snugly as he curled over my back, hiding me from sight. He was murmuring something—the same thing over and over, with small variants—in my ear with a deep, rumbling voice.

I knew the cadence and the tone, if not the words. As a kid, I had a lot of nightmares. My dad, the big, tough former military soldier, would cradle me in the dark when I screamed myself awake and tell me, "It's all right, baby girl. It's all right. Don't be scared. I'll protect you." I was currently encased in a similar shield of muscle and determination. Tears stung my eyes as a trickle of relief ran through me.

A bright-white light burned down at us, shining through my eyelids so I blinked them open and squinted against it in confusion. It threw every leaf and branch above us into high contrast, silhouettes bejeweled with faint gleams of green and backlit by an eye-searing glare. Then the searchlights passed, and that strange flickering fan of green light swept back and forth over the place where we were hiding.

I could feel it on my skin as it licked past, faintly electric, making the hairs on my forearms stand up. It moved over us three times before the sound of the vehicles changed pitch and moved on.

Once the sound had faded into the distance, Teken huffed out all his breath in a sigh, then relaxed his grip on me. I remained right where I was, wishing he would just stay like that and hold me until my blood didn't feel like ice water. He gently stroked his hand over my hair, murmuring those same phrases again.

Finally, the sound moved far enough away that we both heaved sighs of relief. I finally straightened and tilted my head back against Teken's chest so he could look down into my face. My cheeks were wet. I was sure the rest of my makeup was gone, but I managed a smile.

"Thank you," I said softly.

He smiled back.

CHAPTER 15

TEKEN

EVEN AS WE RODE ALONG, dodging the air patrols, the need to kiss and soothe her surged through me.

She's my female, my sheleki.

But similar to the drug she had been pumped full of, the pheromones of our kiss would start my mating frenzy. The last thing we needed right now was to end up frantically mating in the middle of a dangerous jungle with catchers all around, searching for us.

From what I'd been told, the mating urge could very easily overwhelm my common sense. I didn't know what it would do to a human, but I suspected Ella would be left just as vulnerable. But I couldn't deny my burning attraction to her. And my primal need to prove to her that I was a worthy mate burned through my veins.

When the hover squad's engines faded from earshot entirely, it was time for us to rest. We stopped by a narrow creek that ran over rounded crystal stones, and I swung down from behind her, landing boots first in the water with a slight splash.

"Come," I said out of habit as I held out my arms to her. She gave me a blank look, so I curled and uncurled my hands, making a come-hither gesture.

She nodded in response, faint smile returning, and braced herself on my upper arms as she stepped down. I caught her in my lower arms, and she let out a little yelp and started laughing. That made me smile again. I bounced her very lightly, and she squeaked. Then I put her down, and she looked back up at me with a brighter expression than she had worn since I'd met her.

It made me feel warm inside in ways I wasn't accustomed to. Perhaps some of the younger Gladiators would have teased me for that, but I found I did not care. It felt too good and energizing to worry that my gentler emotions might rob me of my warrior's edge.

I led her to the water's border, Brax padding beside us. Crouching, I inspected my reflection under the moonlight, wincing when I saw I was still wearing the ridiculous wig. I worked my fingertips under the scalp piece and pried it loose bit by bit until I could remove the wig altogether.

Ella made a sound that held both relief and approval as I shook my real hair free from under it, stroking my short white-blond spikes back into place. "Better, eh?" I asked her, amused. "I think so, too."

She considered me for a moment, face very thoughtful, then nodded. "Better." She stumbled over the word in my language, but I understood it.

My eyebrows rose. She was clever and learning fast. We were trading words at every opportunity, slowly learning each other's language. Her pronunciation was terrible, and I was sure my attempt at earthling speech was horrible, too. But we had a few shared concepts down now, perhaps twenty words, and a handful of short phrases.

As I watched, she moved carefully past

me and crouched at the water's perimeter to examine some of the jewels. She lifted one precious stone the size of a *threep* egg and the same bright blue. It took up both palms, and she stared at it in wonder, lifting it to let the light of the single visible moon shine through it.

I moved back a little, and Brax bounded past me and splashed into the shallows, then started to slurp up water. His happy wagging sent up plumes of water we both had to duck. She eeked and laughed. I grinned but kept a wary eye out as I walked over to Brax to dig into his saddlebags for my sword and other gear. Even with the catchers distracted searching another part of the forest, the wild-lands were never truly safe.

I felt much more myself when I had my cuirass and cloak back on and my blades at hand again.

I had to keep the energy pistol at the ready, but I felt far better dressed as a Gladiator. Putting away the bits of my disguise Ella was not currently wearing, I reached into the pack, digging out some rations. It wasn't much —just pressed disks of dried meat and green fruit that was bland but very nutritious. I pulled out the water purifier as well. Once I was done, I came back to the water's lip to join her.

Ella was looking around in quiet wonder. The evening had deepened enough that all the stars had come out, and as she crouched next to me at the shore, she spoke low and sweetly to me with unknown words that spurred a deep vein of longing inside me again, aching like a wound.

I offered her some disks and then bent to fill the purifier's cylinder. Flipping on the decontaminator, which bathed the water in bluish light, I let it cycle for a minute. She took an experimental taste of the disks and then proceeded to consume both rations in several large bites. I wondered if the slavers had underfed her on top of everything else, and I handed over one of my own disks without hesitation. She wavered before taking it, then nodded her thanks and devoured that one as well. The water purifier gave a soft chirp, and its light turned off. I retrieved it, then extended the straw for her to sip from.

Apparently, she's dehydrated, too, I thought as I went back to refill the cylinder under a minute later.

I chewed my disk and drank some water, then turned to her, deciding to use gestures to try to get my meaning across more quickly. Pointing at the sky in the direction the hovercraft had gone, I said slowly, "The catchers will come back if they do not find anything farther on. We can only rest here for a little while."

The catchers' expertise was hunting and capturing whoever the Omers sent them after.

Her smile faded slightly, and she gave me that confused look again before nodding grimly. "Slaver scum... search," she hissed.

I nodded enthusiastically. "Yes. *Tagah* search. We run soon." I patted Brax's side for emphasis.

She did understand, enough to hurry through the makeshift meal, sticking close to me while Brax drank water, ate meat disks, and slept for a little while.

After I ate another disk and drank more water, my stomach suddenly felt queasy with mild but all-pervasive worry.

What will I do if she refuses me and does not accept our mate bond? Or gets homesick and wants to go back to Earth?

Not that I had the means to send her back

home. The only beings that had the capability were the slavers that abducted her. Asking the Omers slavers to transport her back to Earth was not an option. Knowing the Omers, they would just agree, then take Ella to another planet to sell her to another race of aliens.

No. She would have to understand there was no going back to Earth. *But what if she becomes unhappy and turns away from me?*

"No," I muttered to myself. Once she and I could communicate clearly, I was certain I could convince her to stay with me. *I have to.* She was my mate, and I'd do anything for her —fight, die, kill, even betray my mission.

The mating urge within me was strong. It felt as though I were waiting for a lost limb to be grafted back on, some essential part of me that wasn't yet returned to me but was at least close.

My Wulfaen was agitated and wanted to claim Ella right now. *But how do earthlings recognize their mates when they do not have inner beasts to make the mating selection? Is this why the slavers conditioned the hostesses? To mimic how the Wulfaen choose their mate? Did the Omers worry that because these females did not have a beast, they wouldn't rec-*

ognize their one true mate, even if he were brought before them?

Gladiators had been taught that their sheleki would be one of their own—and most males would be disappointed with an earthling as a mate. I didn't much care that Ella didn't have an inner beast to bond to my Wulfaen, as long as I could win her heart.

Communicating with Ella would have been much easier if I hadn't left my all alien languages translator back home. That was one mistake I would never make again.

As we rested by the little creek and Brax wandered around sniffing at everything and occasionally coming over to beg for a ration disk, Ella leaned against me suddenly, laying her cheek against my shoulder. I sat very still for a moment and then dared to settle an arm around her shoulders.

She didn't pull away, and I caught myself beaming like an idiot. I quickly hid it behind a more serious expression, scanning around again. This forest was full of dangers. I couldn't afford to focus all my energy on her... as wonderfully easy as it would be.

She was talking. I listened attentively, searching for familiar words, cadences, and tones. Trading languages was almost a lost art on post-translator worlds, and ours was no different. But she was a very expressive human, her face animated, gestures illustrative, and eyes bright and full of emotion. Her dialect was still strange to me, but languages had rules, as I had learned when I was younger during my many grammar lessons. I would have to sort out her Earth words.

Given time, once we had enough of a grasp of the other's language, we would start to help one another bridge the verbal communication gap. But until then, it would be awkward to get our point across. Fortunately, she was making it easier just by being her.

But I couldn't really comprehend anything of what she was currently saying. When she had cried in my arms before, I had understood she was overwrought from her experiences. But right now, she was chattering on excitedly about—something. I tilted my head slightly and then noticed Brax had come over and was doing pretty much the same thing.

Ella noticed our intent stares at the exact same moment and stopped midsentence, then started to laugh.

Oh, wonderful, she thinks I'm as stupid as the dog.

But when I sighed heavily, she just chortled harder, gave me a side hug, and then patted me affectionately as she spoke chirpy-sounding words again.

What in the galaxy does "cyoot" mean?

Whatever else was true, it was clear she was not making fun of me. In fact, she seemed a bit charmed, and that was a very good sign.

Alpha. Don't get too comfortable. The warning from my trainers came back to me at once, even before Brax tensed and pricked up his ears. I looked over at him, touching Ella's shoulder to get her attention. "What is it, Brax?"

Brax started to growl low in his throat.

Suddenly, I heard the hoverbikes again, and this time, they were coming toward us much faster. "The tree line," I shouted, and as Ella jumped up, I grabbed her hand, pulling her in that direction.

We ran. She stumbled a little on the broken ground, and finally, I scooped her up, racing toward the tree line with her in my arms. Brax ran right after us, panting along on my heels.

We had barely managed to dive into the bushes and hunker down out of sight when a trio of the bikes came sweeping down the creek's course, just an arm's length above the surface, sending the water flying in a fine, hard spray to either side. I caught sight of the figures sitting atop the bikes and squinted, trying to make them out beyond the glare of their lights.

Just as I thought... The Omers's slave catchers.

As Ella crouched next to me, I saw the one in the middle clearly as he slowed to look around at the faintly disturbed ground of our camp. I tensed, wondering if I had accidentally left anything behind. But all he did was shine his searchlight on the small stack of bright stones Ella had made.

I studied him, one hand on my pistol. He was almost as tall as I, with a mane of golden-blond hair that was the most natural-looking thing about him. I quickly recognized what he was—a cyborg. His flesh was encased in heavy machine armor, implants ran up both sides of his neck like buttons, his face was covered by a battle mask, and both of his lower arms had been replaced with heavy-duty cyberlimbs bristling with probes, devices—and a pair of weapon barrels. His eyes were a pair of red pinpricks in the blank mask.

Across his back, he had an enormous customized energy cannon, so heavy-looking that it couldn't possibly be fired by anyone without cyberenhancements.

I narrowed my eyes. As soon as I could get an encrypted uplink without having to worry about being tracked, I could look up this cyborg and sort out what I was dealing with. The problem was I couldn't even so much as contact my pack for backup right now without my communication being tracked by the slavers and catchers.

The cyborg catcher sat there for a few moments longer, frowning thoughtfully down at the little pile of stones as his men swept green scanning lights over the banks. Finally, the cyborg turned his head and called to his team, "Anything?"

"Plenty of biotraces, but they could be animals. We can't differentiate anything in this mess, sir." The soldier who spoke immediately looked a little nervous as he admitted his failure.

This confirmed that the cyborg with the

mane of golden-blond hair was their leader.

"Not good enough," the cyborg barked. "We keep looking. If they didn't take the flight corridors, a teleporter, or the waterways, he's traveling overland toward one of the Gladiator sectors. So we search the forest." I couldn't see the man's scowl behind his mask, but I could hear it and the dogged determination in his hard tone.

Both his companions looked at each other, shocked. The second one spoke up. "But, Belland—sir—" he pleaded, only to fall immediately silent when the cyborg glared at him.

Belland. I committed the name to memory.

"If you have a legitimate alternate course of action, speak up now. Otherwise, keep quiet and continue doing your job." Belland's voice was a heavy, metallic rasp, dripping with disdain.

"What about blockading all paths leading into the nearest sector so they can't get in?" the first soldier mused.

"Maybe," Belland snapped, reaching under the edge of his mask and scratching his stubbled skin. "Let's check in with the others around dawn."

Once the three had taken off out of sight, Ella heaved a huge sigh, sagging against me. I held her with one arm, watching them very warily. My hand stayed on my energy pistol until he vanished down the creek with his cronies. Then I slowly got to my feet, helping her up beside me.

"They'll be watching every route between here and my sector," I muttered to her, as much to sort out my own thoughts as to strategize.

Ella and I would have to hide out for a while until I could safely get a message to my pack, or maybe, given time, this Belland cyborg would think we'd been eaten by something out here in the woods and give up chasing us.

"Ella, we need to find a place to hide."

I had an area in mind that might serve—a massive stone outcrop, like a natural fortress, that was riddled with caves, some of which I'd used as camps during training exercises in the past. It was half a day from here. She and I could get there by dawn if we hurried.

Grimly, I swung into Brax's saddle and offered Ella a hand up. It was time to get moving again.

CHAPTER 16

ELLA

THE FOREST'S nightlife was unlike anything I had ever seen. Luminous mushrooms and beetles with glowing bodies flashed past as we rode, their gleams coming in a dozen colors—red, green, blue, gold, white, lavender, orange, pink—some of them solid, some spotted or striped.

I wished I could stop and enjoy the light show, but we were too busy running for our lives. I didn't know where Teken was having Brax take us, but I prayed it was someplace safer than the creek had turned out to be. At least we had managed to stop long enough for me to drink some water and fill my belly with whatever that spicy jerky stuff was.

After leaving the creek, we ran. Brax seemed tireless and moved even faster than before, but he never smacked into or fell over anything.

Does he see in the dark? How well?

I could barely see the faint glow from the sky trickling between the branches, and that was it. But he was as steady in his course, as if it were broad daylight.

We were on our way toward a small clearing in the middle of the thickest brush when something lunged out toward us from behind a tree. I screamed, getting a faint impression of four massive, outstretched claws, a flat head, and skin covered in cockroach-colored scales before we passed it up and it missed its grab.

"What the fuck was that?" I squeaked incredulously as Teken kept a firm grip on me. He rumbled something I couldn't comprehend, and I sighed.

We sure have a long way to go before we can learn a thing about each other beyond the very basic.

But it was clear now why we never *walked* anywhere in this damn forest. Slow movement gave predators a chance to move in on us. And apparently, this forest was full of them.

If I had managed to make it out of the complex alone, this homicidal salad would have eaten me alive by now. The realization alarmed me more than just a little. If the jungle was this dangerous, leading the entire group of stolen women would require a lot more heavily armed help.

Maybe Teken had lots of Gladiators. But until he found some way of reaching them, it was as good as if they didn't exist.

I struggled to catch my breath and fight down panic. The thing that had come after us so quickly would cause as much trouble for the slavers as for us, if not more so. Especially since they made a huge amount of noise when they went anywhere and didn't seem to be very accustomed to forests at all.

Maybe they'll all be eaten by monsters and we can go visit a damn spa somewhere. I squeezed my eyes shut and buried my face in Brax's fur again.

Given the crazy situation, I hated to admit it, but even though we were desperate fugitives right now, I was starting to feel distracted by Teken's closeness again. Not just his muscled chest against my back or his four arms bracing me on either side or his scent in my nostrils.

Every time the dog bounded over a fallen tree limb or picked up a burst of speed, I felt his enormous hairy body jolt me back against Teken. My ass, which took up a nice, thick bit of room on any seat, kept bouncing against his crotch and the insides of his thighs. It felt nice, but it wasn't my body's reaction to the sensation that was distracting me. It was Teken's. I didn't realize it until the sound of the hoverbikes had faded away entirely and we kept bounding along to try to get well ahead of them. Only then, as Brax jumped a silvery stream that bubbled with sudden violence as he leaped over it, did I hear my protector let out a soft, agonized grunt.

For a moment, I worried he had hurt himself somehow or, worse, that I had, knocking into him like that—even though his crotch was armored and my ass nicely padded. But then I felt the shudder run all the way through his body and remembered how he'd agonized before spraying the aphrodisiac's antidote into my face.

A faint grin spread my lips as I hung on,

paying attention to his responses. The poor alien was acting like either he had a big crush on me or he hadn't gotten laid in way too long. Possibly both.

That made me grin even wider. I just couldn't help it. I started letting myself buck against him a little more, not enough to hurt my back or jostle either of us seriously, but enough that my round rump bounced a little harder against his thighs.

He groaned through gritted teeth, and I laughed silently to myself. *Damn. Somebody really does have it bad for little old me. Now that's just adorable.*

He had controlled himself when I was sex crazy from the drug. And I was glad he knew that fucking someone who is effectively help-less is wrong. But my lightly teasing Teken, an alien I'd be happy to hop into bed with—if we weren't fleeing for our lives—was carefree fun.

Hell, truth be told, if there's a remote possi-bility of me dying soon by the hands of the slavers or creepy things in this forest, I might as well enjoy life while I can.

My thoughts snapped back to our journey when I caught sight of a bluish glow up ahead that looked too damn bright to be natural.

Teken slowed Brax and touched my shoulder, his palm engulfing it as he pointed with another hand. The rolling syllables that spilled out of his mouth made no sense, but his tone was full of warning.

He stopped Brax soon after and pointed first at me and then at the dog. "Ella. *Sola iemnon.*"

"Yeah, stay with the dog. I get it." Though, mostly from his body language. Still, it was nice that I was picking up some of his language, even under stress.

I made no move to dismount, only sitting back and stretching. Teken nodded and then, to my surprise, disappeared into the brush.

How someone so huge could vanish so completely and make so little noise, I had no idea. It made me a little nervous. *But if he can practically disappear in front of me, he can probably scout whatever is ahead without getting caught.* I hoped.

Brax sat, panting serenely, and I slid down his side onto the forest floor to stretch my legs properly. Then I leaned against his furry side, trying to calm down. This alien jungle suddenly seemed even huger, darker, and more intimidating now that Teken had gone scouting.

Brax nuzzled my shoulder and then chuffed into my hair, leaving a wet nose print on my cheek.

"Yuck. You're really just a giant drool factory, aren't you?" I whispered, stroking him gently. Right now, aside from the soft sound of my own voice, the dogasaurus rex here was the only roughly familiar thing around.

Especially when a glowing beetle the size of my head went buzzing past, chased by something with four leathery wings and a lashing whip tail. I cringed back against the dog, who sneezed and snuffled after the creatures as they bumbled off through the tree branches above.

"Shit, nothing bothers you, does it?" I muttered as the gigantic lightning bug and small flappy dragon thing disappeared into the dark.

Brax flopped down on his belly with a doggy yawn, content to wait for his master. Maybe he wasn't just a big puppy after all, because he was handling this crazy place a lot more calmly than I was. Of course, it probably helped that he was as big as a pickup truck and had teeth as long as my hand.

How did these aliens end up with dogs anyway?

Brax was too huge, his teeth were wrong, and he seemed too intelligent, but he acted like a canine.

He looked like a dog. He had a moist snoot, a slobbery mouth, and floppy ears. He even had that slightly rank damp dog smell from bounding through the wet rainforest for half the night.

Maybe the slavers had kidnapped more than humans when they abducted Earth's inhabitants. Perhaps they'd taken dogs, birds, and plants.

Ugh, I could really use a shot of vodka right about now.

My nerves were a mess after everything I'd been through—being rescued by a stranger, only to find us both hunted and desperate in the middle of the jungle. But I was glad to have Brax's cuteness and Teken's pure heroic alien hotness around to distract me.

Now, if only Teken would bring his ass back here. Preferably with good news, even if I couldn't understand it.

CHAPTER 17

TEKEN

I HAD to get us to the caves before dawn, when we would lose the cover of shadow.

When I'd spotted the unusual light, I was certain the cyborg had sent scouts ahead. It could be no one else. The slavers were territorial and considered the rainforest to be theirs for many miles around. Even the most daring hunters and herb gatherers would not venture this far into their territory. Anyone who did and wasn't there to pass through to the outposts as quickly as possible was as good as dead.

I moved toward the glow, staying low, aware of male voices up ahead. One of them was the one called Belland, surprising me. I despised the cyborg for his employers, but I had to respect his choice to ride out with his own men instead of directing them by remote.

His tone was cold and tense. I crept forward through the brush, trying my best to get within earshot.

Finally, I found myself on the upper lip of a small canyon, the brush overhanging it hiding me from sight from the hoverbike below. It looked like Belland was taking a report from one of his lieutenants on his communicator. I couldn't see the glowing screen from my perch, but I could hear the voice that came from it just as I could hear his.

Then Belland barked, "I want to know what your leads are on the thief, not your opinions on my search plans. The earthling he took is valuable Omers property." His voice was a low, metallic growl, completely empty of pity or patience.

"His information all leads back to the Capitol, sir, as I said. The only new development is that we can't trace the dog." The voice was a little tinny and hollow sounding coming from the transmitter. "Our intel says they are wild beasts that are native to these woods."

Belland rolled his one good eye. "Great!"

he spat. "Another problem to contend with. There's more than one of those cursed dogs out here."

"Yes, sir," the voice said on the other end of the commlink. "At any rate, that beast will be the only dog in the woods wearing gear, so he'll be easier to find."

I made a mental note of his point.

"Good." The cyborg scoffed. "Now back to the thief. He can't be a noble. Every one of those pompous elites has bottomless expense accounts. The only thing that makes sense is that he's an imposter with no coins who pretended to be a member of a noble family. I just can't figure out why he'd risk being hunted down and killed."

The only positive thing I'd learned from their conversation was that my cover hadn't been blown thus far, which was the best news I'd heard all night. Let them keep thinking I was some idiot thief who was stumbling around the woods, trying to make my way to the outposts.

"We can't cover the entire damn jungle," Belland finally admitted grudgingly. "We'll cover the roads and all near destinations. The

Capitol, Vekim, the trade road, Shore Landing... What am I forgetting?"

"Wulfaen Gladiator territory," a member uttered. "Sector three."

When he mentioned my home and pack, I stiffened, my heart sinking.

Belland grunted. "That's a little bit far. Besides, I heard the Gladiators are an inhospitable lot of barbaric, filthy animals that only care about fighting each other like savages."

His ignorance and insult to my brethren made me grip my sword hilt. For a few moments, I had to fight not to leap off the cliff top and drive my sword into the still-human part of his skull.

I got myself together after several teeth-grinding seconds, but I made another mental note to find a way to separate this half-metal bastard from his life before my mission was over. Not just for what he was and what he was doing, but for flapping his accursed mouth.

"The Gladiators are more concerned about helping their own," Belland remarked. "And they keep to themselves. But I can't go back to the Omers and tell them we deliberately overlooked a possible hiding place for our fugitives."

"Yes, sir." Another soft cough. "Your orders?"

"Stay away from Gladiator lands. Those animals are too territorial. We'll post patrols around their sector. Just try to stay out of their view. We don't want to start a war with them, especially when the Omers are trying to lure them into doing business with them."

Patrols around my sector? This is bad news.

Ella and I would have to hide in the caves until the catchers either gave up or I found a way to sneak past them.

I closed my eyes, trying to focus.

I must get a warning to my pack that the slavers are sniffing around our territory. There had to be a way to alert my brethren. And I would find one, no matter what it took.

Slowly and carefully, I made my way back to Ella, not entirely sure in which direction the slave catcher would fly off. I doubted the cyborg would be able to spot me, but I didn't want to take any chances with Ella's safety.

Ella. I had no idea how I was going to communicate to her that our next few hours would be rough. We would have to make it to the caves before dawn and wait out the slave catchers, since trying to bypass the area they were searching was too risky and relied on guesswork.

I scowled, thinking about a night alone with her, trying to resist the urge to coax her into sex. This was not a matter of a simple coupling out of sheer attraction. If I went too far with my true mate, even as much as a kiss, I was done, and my primal urge to claim and mark her would overtake any rational thought. If I resisted, my Wulfaen would rise to take over. And if that happened, nothing would keep me from completely losing myself to lust until I caught enough of my own scent on her skin and inside her womanhood to know she was claimed by both the Gladiator and Wulfaen.

The mating frenzy was part of the reason that sex with our female was a private, intimate affair. Casual rutting was just scratching the surface of what a Gladiator really desired. The first time with one's own mate was both sacred and carnal.

After marking our sheleki with the mating serum that coated our fangs and permanently leaving our scent on her so other Wulfaen knew she'd been claimed, the mated couple would rut for days, only stopping to eat and catch a few moments of sleep. Then they'd resume fucking until the fire within their loins cooled... slightly.

Once the frenzy flame ebbed, both partners would be sated but too exhausted to do anything but sleep for hours. If that happened, I would have to send Brax back to my pack with a message that I needed help. With Brax gone, we would be left with no guardian while we rested.

Too dangerous. I can't dare touch her.

But what if I lose control, slipping into the mating thrall? Would she understand the primal pull that would surge through my veins? Or would she think I'm just some wild pup that cares about nothing but fucking her? All of those ideas were intolerable.

When I returned, Ella and Brax were safe —*thank the gods*—and relaxing where I'd left them. The only greeting I got from Brax was a thud of his tail, but Ella's reaction was surprising. She jumped up, lunged forward, and threw herself against my chest. I froze at once, stunned and delighted, and hugged her back gently as she spoke low and rapidly in words I didn't understand.

I closed my eyes, cradling her small, soft, lush body against me and feeling my own respond even through a layer of armor. My resolve wavered as I gasped for air.

Too much...

Her being in my arms bombarded me with so many emotions—awe, joy, hope, and ecstasy.

Her chatter took on an urgent, pleading edge as she clung to me. And from her tone and the passionate, intense shake in her voice, I realized she must have been worried about me while I was gone.

I moved back slightly, looking down at her in confusion. I tried to pick out specific words from the jumble and managed a few—the filthy epithet for "slaver" that I always used, Brax's name, my name, "escape." But it was still almost all nonsense to me.

She stood against me lightly, hands sliding up and down my chest as I struggled to ignore just how good her touch felt. This was not the time—and certainly not the place—to become intimate with my mate, especially when doing so would take over too much of my consciousness, making it nearly impossible for me to get us to safety.

Maybe... just one kiss?

I wanted so badly to take her from behind, sinking my serum-coated fangs into the tender nape of her neck and marking her forever as mine.

No. I must resist.

It took everything I had to let go of her and step away completely.

My determination to maintain space between us almost splintered when she made a small, sad sound and I saw first disappointment, then frustration in her eyes.

I shook my head, holding up two of my hands, and spoke in as gentle a tone as I could muster. "I'm sorry, sheleki. I want to, but I cannot. Not while we are still in danger."

She frowned. "Sheleki?" she repeated. It was a word she had not picked up yet.

I nodded and gestured to her. "You're my one true mate."

I knew she didn't understand the great honor my Wulfaen and the gods had bestowed upon me. Now I had something all Gladiators prayed to the gods for—a mate to love, cherish, and protect. It was a gift I wouldn't squander.

She stared back at me and then, to my great relief, simply nodded, moving back over to Brax.

I plodded after her, tired, resigned, and aching with the need for her. I didn't know how I would resist if I needed to, but I would have to find a way.

CHAPTER 18

ELLA

I WAS STARTING to wonder if I had misread signs that Teken was attracted to me.

The alien really seemed to enjoy when I hugged him, but then he backed off immediately, as if I'd embarrassed him or touching him was somehow inappropriate.

Was he turned off by my "please fuck me" shenanigans when I was drugged?

Maybe I make him nervous... Or... he's not sure if my wanting him has something to do with residual effects from the drugs.

How can I let him know that my mind is fucking clear now? That I want him in the most primal, sexual way?

Sighing heavily, I mentally registered that

wanting to have sex with a four-armed alien was so out of character for the "I'm swearing off relationships forever" me. But being abducted from Earth and now fleeing for my life made me realize life was too damn short and tomorrow was not a guarantee.

From now on, I was doing what made me happy, and that included being with an alien Gladiator who made me smile and allegedly turned into some furry animal. I didn't give a shit about the odd combination.

I'm going to enjoy life and the here and now with no regrets.

So how do I get him to understand he has the green light to fuck me senseless?

CHAPTER 19

ELLA

LATER, while we drank water and nibbled on rations, Teken kept a watchful eye on the glow in the distance, as if waiting for it to do something.

I still didn't know where he was taking me. All we had managed to sort out between us was a few words besides our names. He kept pointing off in one direction, past the glow that he had investigated. But I had no idea what was in that direction.

Is it too much to hope that it's a paradise spa with hot, muscular four-armed masseurs in little loincloths?

I remembered all the images I had seen of the beauty of this world as my captors had tried to acclimate me to their planet. I'd even spied a few paradise-level white sand beaches amid all the forests and ultramodern city spires.

Maybe that's where we're going, some-place with welcoming non-predatory or crazy aliens. Shit. I hope so...

But the truth of the matter was I didn't know him at all. Hell, we didn't even speak the same language. Yes, he saved my ass when he could have left me at the mercy of the slavers. But still... how could I be completely sure he wasn't going to fuck me over? Could I trust him, knowing that the Omers were con-ditioning females to sell to his people? Or was there more to the story between the Omers and Gladiators?

And then there was the fact that I didn't understand why he was being so protective and going through so much trouble for me, putting his own life in danger.

Despite his mixed signals, he was at-tracted to me. That much I knew from the way he touched and looked at me. His expres-sive mug would have lost him plenty at poker. But his life was too high a price to pay for liking me.

As we waited until it was safe for us to leave, we were trying to teach each other new words. Much of the time, his expression, tone, and body language were most of what I had to go by as he struggled to communicate with me.

Right now, it was my turn to teach him a bit of English. And I was running into an unexpected bit of trouble. Frustrating, but it was awkward enough to break the tension of waiting with a bit of humor.

I put my hand on my chest. "Woman."

He blinked slowly, puzzlement crossing his face.

I patted my chest again. "Wom-an."

"Wom-an." His brow creased. He seemed confused. He was also now staring right at my tits—which I had always been kind of proud of, but still.

Come on now.

"What is it?" I asked almost reflexively.

He blinked several times. "Ella...?" he asked, still looking at my breasts and then back up at my face in total puzzlement.

I realized where I had laid my hand a moment later and had to fight back an awkward laugh. "No, no."

I swept my hand up and down to take in my whole body. "Woman." Then I pointed at him and made the same sweeping gesture up and down his form. "Man."

I was hoping I wouldn't have to resort to charades here. If I'd accidentally looked like I was introducing him to my rack before, God knows what miscommunications would happen next.

Realization dawned across his rugged features, and he nodded. "Wom-an!" He pointed to me. "Man!" Then he gestured to himself.

I nodded enthusiastically. *Now we're getting somewhere.* And I had managed to get through it without a single pantomimed dick.

He was still staring at my boobs.

I blinked at him and then put my hands on my hips. "Hello?"

He looked up at me hesitantly, then back at them. "Ella?"

I rolled my eyes. "Breasts, Teken."

He perked up. "Breasts!"

That just made me snort and shake my head. "Yeah, you picked that one up real fast."

He was a big, scary extraterrestrial, but he was obviously one of those honorable, warrior types... and he was also kind of a big dork sometimes, like any male. His obvious intention to become besties with my well-endowed cleavage was more amusing as opposed to annoying, but that was because I found everything about him alpha sexy.

But how does he feel about me?

"Do you like me?" I asked.

I didn't know if he had anywhere near the words to answer my question. I tried an approximation in his language, but I might have been babbling about space cabbage for all I knew.

He cocked his head.

I sighed. Our communication issues were going to be a real problem if we didn't figure this shit out quick.

Brax came up behind him and butted his head under Teken's arms like a much smaller dog, tail wagging happily.

I put my hand on Teken's arm. He shivered slightly, muscles tightening, his eyelids sliding down just a bit. His breath went just a touch harsh, and I knew at once that I was right; he was fighting his desire for me.

When he finally, uneasily, pulled away, I said quietly, "Why?"

He blinked several times and looked away, pausing for a long time before looking back at me. He spoke in his own language, slowly, but I could only grasp bits of it with the words we had taught each other so far. "I belong... you... mate."

Wait... what? He thinks I'm his mate?

"Whoa." I held up a hand, smiling to let him know I wasn't offended, then did my best to repeat what he had said back to him. "You belong to me? And I'm a mate?"

He nodded. "Mate. Sheleki."

Does he think I'm his girlfriend?

It was one of the words he kept using—*sheleki*. "Mate" was what he said when I had asked for the meaning.

"I'm not your mate, Teken."

He scowled as if he either didn't understand enough of what I just said or refused to believe it.

He folded both sets of arms across his chest and said in broken bits of English, mixed with his own language, "You are... *sheleki*. I protect you."

Yep... he thinks I'm his girlfriend. My eyebrows went up. He seemed so vehement about me being his sheleki—almost angry.

How did I end up with a damn alien boyfriend?

Then he said something in his own language that I couldn't fully understand, but I got the gist of his words and it startled me.

Did he say, "If I claim you, I cannot protect?" I bit my bottom lip. *Claim? As in I belong to him—no one else?*

Fuck. My. Life. This lack of effective communication thing is going to be the death of me.

He glanced away in what I realized was a gesture of deference—and possibly a touch of self-consciousness.

Yes. There was no mistaking it. Teken thought I was his girlfriend.

I liked him a lot, but I wasn't interested in changing my status from "single" to "in a relationship." Besides, getting attached to Teken would only hurt both him and me when I had to leave him to go back to Earth. But I also knew nothing I said—even if he could understand—would change his mind.

We'd better get out of this forest fast and find me another communication device, because this mate shit is annoying like fingernails on a chalkboard.

"Okay," I replied, giving him a smile to show I wasn't upset with him. There was no need to make waves over this. It could be fixed —hopefully real soon.

His brows drew together again, but the faintest smile curved his lips. I took a few more swallows from his water purifier. I wanted to ask him where we would be going from here, but I was starting to get tired.

I was stifling a yawn when we heard the familiar whine of an engine. The slave catchers were on the move again. Teken shooed me back against the trunk of a tree, then shielded me from sight. Around us, I heard the stirring of foliage as their flying bikes blew past overhead. Then it was gone, finally, and we both heaved a sigh of relief.

"Gone, sheleki. We go." He climbed back on Brax and offered me a hand-up.

"Ella. Not sheleki." I reminded him.

"Yes, sheleki."

Damn stubborn but caring alien. I shook my head as I let him help me into my seat. If he wanted to keep calling me sheleki, I wasn't going to waste a lot of time arguing over it.

Brax took off like lightning once we got on the trail Teken directed him to. The journey was dark, so Brax's eyesight had to be sharp because he kept us from smacking into anything. Teken assisted by ducking us under branches and shielding me from any foliage sticking into our path.

With eyes closed, I bent low over Brax's neck with Teken's muscled torso pressed against my back. Only the comfort of his body kept me from being terrified. All this excitement and drama had exacted its price on me—I was exhausted.

My eyelids snapped open at the faint hissing sound up ahead. Teken stiffened, shouting an order. I glimpsed a shadow shaped like a thick rope or a snake darting past overhead. Brax snarled, leaping aside. Blind in the dark, I hung on and struggled not to panic.

Calm. Keep calm. He will handle it. I'm not about to die.

Dammit. I'm not. Keep calm!

But I was shaking like a leaf.

I could hear more slithering and rustling up ahead, and Brax turned, his claws scratching on stone as he bolted up a steep slope. I heard the rasp of steel on leather as multiple blades were drawn from their sheaths.

"Ella. No move."

I didn't know the next few words he spoke, but they were spat in frustration and disgust.

Teken slashed with two of his arms. I smelled the scent of plant sap, but I also heard a weird, echoing screech from up in the trees.

Brax ran on, dodging and growling, while Teken lashed out with his blades at whatever was attacking us. I tangled my fingers in Brax's coat and hunched down as best I could, trying not to flinch whenever something sticky and chlorophyll-smelling spattered on me.

Are we being attacked by plant monsters?

Finally, the squeals of pain grew louder, and I heard the noisy rustling of something far too animallike to be a plant dragging itself away from us through the brush. Teken panted for breath as he sheathed his blades and then shouted an order to the dog, who changed direction and started running steadily again. There was pain in Teken's voice, and I began to worry.

The sky was starting to lighten by the

time I realized something was very wrong. Teken was panting harshly. Carefully reaching one hand back, I splayed my fingers against his side, feeling that something had torn his armor. As the light brightened, I peeked back and spied a dark wetness seeping through several gashes.

Fuck! He got wounded protecting me.

I was relieved to see that most of the dark stains on his clothes—and mine, in spots—were a greenish sap. His purplish-red blood mixed with it here and there, and he grunted with pain now and again. I wondered about the effects of getting that stuff inside his wounds. I wanted to ask, but nagging him with my concerns while we were still fleeing didn't seem like the right thing to do.

The trees started to thin, and the ground sloped upward. Up ahead, silhouetted against the lightening sky, I saw a gigantic stone outcropping the size of a row of skyscrapers.

"Holy crap, what is that?"

Teken groaned in response and muttered a few orders to the dog in his language, his head drooping over me. I looked over and saw his eyes glazing. I couldn't confirm it in the dim light, but something about his skin looked off—almost paler.

Fat raindrops began spattering us as we made our way up the hill, washing the green crap off us as Brax ran out into the open. This time when Teken groaned, it sounded almost like relief. I looked at him and saw the green stuff had washed from his skin—but as for the blood, every time the rain washed it away, more ran out to stain his skin again.

Oh God. This is bad.

"You're still bleeding!" I called out, alarmed.

He let out a grunt and shook his head to clear it, then straightened. "We stop soon," he rasped, sounding exhausted. Either he had misheard me or misunderstood or hadn't yet picked up enough of the right words in English to reassure me about his injuries.

A massive mound of boulders lay at the foot of the outcrop. Brax started bounding up them, making the steep climb as if he had done it a dozen times before. I had to close my eyes and hang on with both hands, heart pounding, and I prayed Teken would not lose consciousness.

I didn't know where we were headed

until we were almost upon it—the black maw of a cave dug deep into the rock beneath an overhang hung with silvery moss. Brax came to a stop inside and bellied down immediately. Teken collapsed sideways out of the saddle.

I didn't know how I managed to jump down ahead of him to break his fall, but I suddenly found myself barely propping up his mostly limp, massive body. "Oh shit. Teken? Don't faint..."

I punctuated my gasped-out words with grunts of effort as I got him laid down next to Brax. I could barely see anything in the dimness of the cave, but I at least managed to get him onto his side in the recovery position. Thankfully, it was dry in here, even as the rain pitter-pattered down outside.

He shook himself awake a minute later, groaning softly. "Ella."

I moved to his side at once. "What... I do?" I stumbled out in his language, figuring he didn't have energy to spare to try his new bits of English.

"Plant... frees... blood." His voice was slurred as he pointed at the wounds still refusing to clot.

I felt a creeping horror as I started to sort out what he was talking about.

The vine sap is an anticoagulant. No wonder he's still bleeding even though all the scratches I can see look shallow.

I stood and started digging into the saddlebags for anything that looked remotely like a medical kit. I found a small light source—a headband that had a bead on it that glowed to life when poked. I put it on and kept digging. Finally, just as I was starting to get frustrated, Teken let out a grunt and pointed at a flat silver case I'd just pulled out.

Dropping to my knees, I opened it to offer him the contents. His hand wavered hazily over a series of clear tubes inside, each one tipped with flat disks of silver on each end and filled with something that looked like mercury. He grabbed two and then almost dropped them.

I snatched them from him. "Show me." I put my hand around his and let him weakly guide my hand toward the side of his massive neck.

I pressed one against the skin and heard a faint hiss. A moment later, the entire cylinder started draining its contents into him in little bursts in time with his pulse. He sighed and closed his eyes, leaning back against the dog.

The second one he guided to his thigh where the largest gash in his armor exposed a patch of skin so smooth that, for a moment, distracted me from how bad off he was. I emptied the second cylinder into him and watched as, slowly, the edges of his wounds started to gleam silver and pull together.

I stared as each cut and gash closed, voids and patches of missing skin filling in silver. The labored note left his breathing, and after a little while longer, he sighed, some of the color coming back into his face.

"You all right?" I asked, and after staring at me for a few moments, he seemed to at least register the concern in my voice and just smiled.

He stood and said, "Danger gone." Then he followed up with a few unfamiliar words and mentioned Brax before removing the saddlebags from Brax's body. He said something to the dog in a sharp voice. Obediently, Brax trotted over to the far side of the cave, lay down, yawned, and promptly started to fall asleep.

My eyes widened as Teken started to strip off his shredded armor.

My jaw dropped. *Holy shit.*

He was still a damn alien, and the muscles in his massive back were complex and layered, lending strength to both sets of arms. But aside from that and the bluish tinge to his skin, he looked like such a perfect specimen of good old-fashioned masculinity, and all I could do was stand there and stare at him.

In the faint light, I gawked at his massive shoulders, heavily muscled back, and amazingly sculpted ass barely covered by a clinging loincloth.

He turned to me. "Ella. Need heal... more. Need Wulfaen. Stay. No run."

I arched a brow. *Run from what?*

I watched in fascination while he stripped off his loincloth and boots. The air around his big body seemed to shimmer with an almost imperceptible iridescence, and in that moment, Teken was gone and in his place was a huge silver wolf.

"Shit. This is some freaky shit," I muttered, my heart racing like I'd just run a marathon.

He looked just as intimidating and big in

wolf form with his powerful build, heavily muscled neck, and robust limbs.

He stepped forward.

I shrieked, throwing my arms out protectively. Then I stood frozen. I was afraid to move, afraid to breathe, and when the wolf made a hesitant move toward me, I shrank back, keeping my eyes fixed on him.

"No. Stay," I said shrilly, pointing at the creature, trying to sound firm, though my heart was pounding in my chest.

The wolf stepped back, then sat down. He whined, cocking his head to one side and studying me. He was a big animal, but he didn't seem inclined to attack me.

What are you talking about, Ella? This is Teken. He won't hurt me.

I beckoned the wolf with my fingers. I laughed when he went down on his belly and began edging closer. He covered those last remaining steps between us, and then his pink tongue came out and washed over my fingers.

"Ew."

I carefully stretched out my arm, letting just the tips of my fingers stroke his massive head. His fur was thick and shiny, silver just like Teken's hair.

His Wulfaen is strong and beautiful.

Reminding me of Brax, he butted my hand gently with his massive head, pushing against my touch. He seemed to be encouraging me to stroke him with a firm pressure. I looked into the wolf's intelligent eyes, and my heart missed a beat.

Fuck... I'm falling for him.

"Teken," I croaked. "I need you not to be a wolf... I mean... Wulfaen right now."

He seemed to understand my request. The air began to faintly shimmer, and then Teken the alien stood before me, breathing hard.

"Teken? Are you okay?"

He nodded.

Now I understood the difference between the "Gladiator"—the alien—and "Wulfaen"— the beast. Those were his two forms.

"So that is your Wulfaen?"

"Yes," he acknowledged. "Ella no scared?"

I touched his cheek. "Ella no scared."

Turning his head quickly, he pressed his lips against my palm.

My clit pulsed from his touch. *Yep. I'm definitely starting to have feelings for him.* Needing a distraction, I pulled away, then crouched to dig dutifully in his saddlebags, coming out with a few travel blankets and one of those silver cloths for cleaning.

He smiled, then took the cleansing cloth from me. I struggled to keep my eyes on his face as he started dragging the cloth all over his skin to cleanse himself.

Oh my. Oh wow. My mouth was suddenly dry as a bone, and my heart pounded in my ears. All of the aliens I had seen were built, but Teken raised the bar unbelievably.

I kept trying not to let my eyes wander but failed epically. He was not only sexually compatible with humans, but also damn hung by any standards.

His smooth skin was covered with faint scars, some showing only in a slight shift in texture and sheen, but they just enhanced his good looks and made him look like a total badass.

He didn't have a hair on his body below his eyebrows, from what I could see—which was a lot. Either he waxed diligently or Gladiators were just less hairy than humans. Combined with his sleek, short hair and the stripes and dots of black crossing his skin in a dozen places, it made him look both alien and like a beautiful piece of art. With great disappointment, I watched as he donned his loincloth, then his boots.

Teken's every move looked painful as he went through his packs, digging out several boxes, a roll of cloth, and a length of silvery rope. I helped him as much as I could, taking each item and setting it aside in a pile for him.

He found another one of the headbands and put it on, then handed me a packet of dried meat. "For Brax," he grunted.

At the mention of his name, the dog's eyes slid open. Striding over to him, I patted the dog before feeding him the circles of dried meat.

I kept taking peeks of Teken as he moved around the cave, which was a little low-ceilinged for him, forcing him to crouch. With his four arms, he could get a lot done in a short time. He didn't bother grabbing for clothes. Instead, he started setting up our hidden camp in just the loincloth and his boots. It was a look I wished he'd keep from now on, even though it wouldn't be practical for wandering around in a jungle full of monsters.

I wanted him. But I also knew that Teken wanted me to be his "mate."

Can I give him what he wants without losing my heart in the shuffle?

I didn't have the answer to that question because I'd been ducking and hiding from serious relationships for so long that I didn't even know if I had it in me to be either mate or girlfriend material. But I liked Teken more than any male I'd ever met. And given everything I'd been through at the hands of my abductors and we'd been through while dodging the catchers, I concluded that life was about taking chances. And guarding my heart was wasting precious time that I could be enjoying with my Wulfaen Gladiator.

So for however long I remained on this planet, I was willing to give Teken my all because my big, protective alien had earned it.

CHAPTER 20

TEKEN

THE FANGVINE ALMOST KILLED ME. Gods... it almost killed all of us.

I'd been so distracted by Ella and the catchers hunting us that I'd forgotten that the horrid fangvine became more mobile when a rainstorm hit. I was usually the master of anything the jungle threw at me, especially with a fleet-footed riding dog and being heavily armed and properly trained. Dodging slave catchers while protecting my mate in the blackest part of the night, however, made things a bit more difficult. And I had paid for my inattention.

The whole ride over to the caves, only

Ella and my need to get her to safety had kept me conscious and hanging on for dear life.

Once we'd made it to safety, I thought two vials of nanites would be enough to take over the duties of some of my missing blood cells, stop the bleeding, and clean the wounds of contaminants, including that damned anticoagulant sap. But I was hurt worse than I thought, and I needed to shift into my Wulfaen to quicken the healing process.

I smiled just remembering how, eventually, Ella accepted my Wulfaen, and her bravery made both my Gladiator and inner beast joyful and proud.

I was still suffering from a headache and dizziness from the blood loss, and I was so thirsty. I set up the rain catcher just outside the cave mouth. It took three units of purified water before my belly filled and I didn't feel thirsty anymore.

After a lot of struggling around our language barrier, Ella had assisted me with setting up the portable nest. It was a gift from the elders, a rapid-collapse model that allowed me to sleep in comfort. Normally suspended from the trees, the tented structure, with its heavily padded bottom and doughnut-shaped sides, now took up the back half of the cave. Its faint bluish glow helped make the place look a bit more like a camp and less like a desperate hiding place.

Brax stuck his head out into the rain and slurped at the droplets as he kept watch for us. It was still dark and he was camouflaged against the damp volcanic rock, so I knew he wouldn't be spotted, especially now that I had taken off his harness.

I knelt stiffly to fill the purifier a last time for Ella. I could hear her humming some-where near the nest. My thighs ached slightly as I straightened, turning to bring her a drink. I stopped short, eyes wide. My loincloth was getting almost painfully tight.

Oh gods, give me strength!

She had grabbed a bathing cloth and stripped down to get rid of the sweat and sap all over her. With her back to me, she stood, running the cloth over every curve of her mag-nificent body while I stared at her.

I looked down at myself, naked except for a loincloth and my boots—and the loincloth was doing nothing to hide my desire for her.

I wondered if she had found the view of my body just as distracting as what stood across the room from me now, lit by that soft blue glow, dark skin shimmering. Her easy, musical voice hummed tunelessly in time with the strokes of the cloth across her body. When she turned halfway and lifted her arm so her breasts rode high and her back arched, I wanted to go sprinting toward her and kiss her hard.

The clothes the slavers had left her in were revealing enough, but this... was a whole different level. She was so small and soft and rounded that all four of my hands itched with the urge to caress her.

How can she be so beautiful yet so strange at the same time?

She had only one set of hands, which were soft and fragile. I would have to be careful with her. Though, she had already proven that she was tough and nearly fearless.

Now how can I convince her we belong together when we only have a few dozen words in common?

Taking a deep breath, I turned to my armor, which needed treatment as well. The fangvine had made a complete mess of it, compromising my protective covering in several spots. If I did not repair the gashes, a lucky shot or a nanotech bullet would penetrate it easily.

Ignoring my aching erection and the sweet feminine humming and rustling behind me, I set to work laying the armor on a rock outcrop and grabbing my repair kit. The repair bots were small, spidery things, barely larger than the bond-filament thread spool they carried, but they started sewing up the slits in my armor as soon as I set each one in place.

Gladiators lived simply, but we weren't stupid. Any technology that directly improved our ability to do our duty and survive was encouraged, and we were allowed a few other luxuries as well. My sector was not like one of the tall, sharp-pointed cities where the Omers and nobles lived, with their technological miracles fueling endless excesses. But those who lived in my pack had access to military-grade healing and repair technologies. Without repair abilities, my warriors and I would be sunk in the field. The jungle chewed up gear and spat it out in pieces—and often did the same to its owners.

I did my best to focus on repairing my armor rather than the gorgeous sight I kept glimpsing in the corner of my eye. She was like a goddess as her body moved sensually while she cleaned herself.

I resolved not to succumb to her seductive scent and body. But I couldn't trust myself. I focused on directing the little spiders to patch my armor, seamlessly sewing shut the tough polymer-reinforced hide with tiny sutures. Normally, watching them fascinated me— how they could erase the signs of a battle with their tireless tending, just as the nanites were now doing to my flesh.

I was exhausted. The rain was really starting to pound outside the cave mouth, which delighted me in a few ways. It would cover any potential tracks, and it would make for a terrible time for those trying to find us. Maybe it would even trickle into some of that cyborg's fancy mods and give him trouble.

But the hiss of the rain and the blast of warm, wet air it brought with it left me even more spent than my day and my wounds. I couldn't bring myself to do much more than shove some rations in my face and put together a portion to bring to Ella once she was... dressed.

When I finally turned back around, she was done and had pulled on my tunic. She was just curling up against the padded wall of the nest, the side slit of the tunic revealing the whole smooth curve of her hip and part of one buttock. I stopped at the nest entrance and swallowed, my mouth feeling very dry.

She looked up at me sleepily and smiled, saying something I didn't understand at all in a husky voice. Looking away quickly, I bent down to take off my boots, ignoring the way my cock pushed obstinately against my belly.

Be strong, I told myself, but inside, I wondered if I could.

She asked me that same question she had before, seeming puzzled by my lack of reaction to her pretty obvious invitation. I settled in beside her, facing her, not quite at arm's length. I offered her the food and drink instead of answering, and she ate and drank with a gleam in her eye that told me she had been wanting for both.

I had to explain to her—as best I could—why I could not bed her. But my grasp of her language was so lacking, and I was so tired. So instead, I acted, letting that speak for me. I laid my head against the ring and felt the material reshape to conform to and support it. My body ached with need for her, but it also ached with fatigue.

She reached over, brushing her fingertips against my cheek where one of the clusters of nanites was hard at work.

"Sleep?" she managed in my language, and I nodded and yawned.

The last thing I felt before dropping unconscious was the sudden warm, soft weight of her body curled against my back.

My dreams were a muddled mix of sensual treats—memories of Ella's desperate and drugged kisses, the sight of her nude body behind the veil wall of the nest.

I gasped awake, the soft blue glow and the rattle of the rain a fresh shock to my tattered nerves. For a few seconds, all I could feel was the throbbing ache in my groin and the deep frustration I couldn't shake. Then I felt Ella curled up against my chest, and I froze.

All four of my arms had wrapped around her in sleep, and my face was buried in her hair. She breathed softly, head pillowed against me, and didn't stir as I lifted my head to look around.

Brax had wandered into the nest as well and had flopped down on the other side, snoozing. Judging by the fair amount of light coming in, it was late morning. I had much more sleeping to do before I would be truly well, but old habits dragged me up to check on things.

Pulling away from Ella took a lot of self-control, but I knew if I didn't, the inner restraint would melt away like ice in my fists. I stood and walked past Brax. He twitched an ear but didn't wake.

I went to the cave mouth and looked out over the jungle. The far-off spires of the slavers' complex gleamed dully in the rain. Now and again, I saw hover vehicles of various sizes flying above the jungle, but there were fewer than I expected. Either that or they were having trouble flying in the rain.

A muffled boom caught my attention. My

head snapped around, and I saw one of the hoverbikes was now missing from the sky and a thin thread of smoke was drifting up from the canopy.

I let out a laugh. "Well! Serves you filth right." Too bad we were in no shape to travel in this mess ourselves. Brax didn't mind the rain and neither did I, but I didn't know about Ella.

I emptied my bladder over the edge and spat in the direction of the crash. I hoped it was the cyborg, overtaxing his vehicle with the weight of all his fancy mods.

The cyborg thought he would fetch Ella back like a piece of property.

Not my sheleki. I will die first—and he will die well before that.

A drink from the purifier later and I plodded back to check on the mate in question. The one who kept insisting she wasn't one. I'd sensed her confusion and doubt when I called her my sheleki. And for the first time in my life, my heart actually felt laden with an invisible weight.

Ella didn't understand the importance of a Gladiator finding his one true mate or the fact that he'd die before ever harming his sheleki. It was instilled from the moment of birth, buried deeply within each male, an instinct to protect and defend, to nurture and cherish his female.

I had to be patient with my mate. And when we were back safely in my pack, I would show her what it was like to be claimed by her Gladiator.

When I settled down next to her, her eyes opened. She smiled softly and rolled over, sitting up a little, her eyes hooded and drowsy, as if she weren't quite awake enough to be fully aware.

"Hey, Teken," she murmured and then leaned up to kiss me.

I froze, anticipating disaster but knowing as well that I couldn't stop her. Nor could I shut down the need to have her. My body flat out refused to pull away in time. My inner beast slid against my skin, prodding me to claim her. She brushed her lips against mine, then deepened the kiss until her mouth was caressing mine passionately.

The kiss mixed sensuality and tenderness, enthralling me and hardening my cock immediately. My mind started to drift away blissfully. My instincts rose in a wave of pleasure and lust, threatening a total takeover.

Pull away, my common sense demanded. I was doomed if I didn't.

I can't.

I pulled her closer—and felt my resolve slip away.

CHAPTER 21

ELLA

KISSING TEKEN for the first time was instinct mixed with desire and curiosity.

Once my lips touched his, he froze for a moment, then got into it, returning my kiss with a sigh that sounded like relief. He was careful, his hands just barely settling on my forearms and back.

Three seconds into the kiss, however, it was like a switch had been flipped. I felt a violent shudder go through him, and his grunt of pleasure became a low growl that amped up into something that sounded almost angry.

He pulled away with a gasp and looked down at me with glazed and dilated eyes. I suddenly remembered the drug I had been given and the way my reflection had shown the same thing. This was what he was experiencing right now—a cloying hunger like I'd felt back at the facility. But I knew no one had drugged Teken. Unless I had somehow, just by kissing him.

I thought of what he had struggled to tell me when we had almost kissed in the forest. It had sounded like a warning.

"I must guard. If I mate, I cannot guard."

I looked up into his glossy eyes and remembered how I had felt when they brought me to his suite. Aching, frenzied, desperate for sex with him. I even saw that same pain in the depths of his eyes now—a craving for satisfaction so deep that it destroyed all focus.

"Ella," he rasped in a low, shaky voice, hands trembling as his grip tightened on me.

I looked him over. He was nearly nude except for that filmy loincloth, which bulged nearly to the point of tearing from the massive erection underneath. He shuddered as I ran a hand down his belly, and his hands flexed against my skin.

"It's okay." I soothed, petting his chest,

sliding my hands over his sides and then down over the bunched muscles of his ass. He jolted and gasped through his teeth, his head rolling back. I tried to use my soft, teasing tone to convey meaning. "Come here. Let the dog keep watch for a while."

I kissed him again, and he caught me in his arms, forcing himself to lie back as if worried he would hurt me if he got too aggressive. I was all for the gentle giant routine until I knew my way around his body; that massive, barely restrained cock I spied would take some careful handling.

I climbed onto his lap, straddled his muscular thighs with mine, and started running my hands over his body. He shuddered, panting through his teeth, head lolling—and then his hands settled on me, fumbling impatiently at the fastenings at the sides of my borrowed tunic. I heard the snaps give just as I was ready to wrestle the whole thing off. He slid his hands under the fabric, two of them running up and down my sides while the others removed the intervening cloth.

I kissed him again, rubbing my breasts on his bare chest, and smiled against his mouth when he started trembling. Then one set of hands slid around to cup them while the other pair slid down, each one grabbing a globe of my ass.

When he set to work on me, kneading and stroking, I gasped. My fingers were still mapping the muscles of his back, but as time wore on and his hands explored me, I started to whimper, using my nails far more than my fingertips.

I had imagined a few times what it would be like to have two sets of his hands caressing me at once. I felt almost overwhelmed by the wash of sensation over my skin. It relaxed me but left me shivering, craving greater intensity even as I softened in his grip.

He seemed almost blind with lust now. When I managed to open my own eyes, I could see him gazing up at me with a tinge of wildness. His lips were parted as he gasped slowly for air. A look of almost panic crossed his features and then vanished.

I tried to say something encouraging, but I lost it and yelped a little as he scooped me up with all four arms.

Sitting up, he lifted me to his mouth, plucking me almost fully off his lap as he ran his lips over my throat and shoulders, then down between my breasts. He nuzzled me, closing his eyes reverently, then ran his tongue over each breast in turn, tasting every inch of my skin.

His movements were quick, hungry, barely restrained. Little purring growls vibrated his lips as they circled my areola and closed briefly over one nipple for a teasing tug. I gasped and then let out a low whimper, my hips rolling reflexively.

Now I was the one panting. I gripped his hair and pressed myself against his face encouragingly while he swirled his tongue over one of my breasts before fastening on my nipple. My back arched. I wrapped my legs around his waist and squirmed against him, hips working frantically.

My voice rose and fell with every pull of his lips. I shimmied my hips against his belly, feeling my cunt ache with the need to be filled as he suckled and caressed me.

Two hands lifted me, the other two kneading my ass and the tops of my thighs. He was so strong. I went almost limp in his arms as he lifted me farther in his powerful grip, and he started kissing his way down my belly. His wide, smooth-lipped mouth and the delicate brush of his sharp teeth were accompanied by a tongue that felt covered in soft ridges.

I didn't realize he had laid me down until my back hit the padded bottom of the tent and his hands gripped my thighs and parted them. With three hands keeping them apart, I couldn't move them, even when he bent down and started running his face over my cunt, nuzzling and kissing.

Holy shit.

In my experience, guys almost never did that, especially as an opener.

My back arched, and my eyes rolled closed. "Ah... oh fucking God, yeah—" And then my voice broke into an inarticulate scream as he parted my pussy lips and started licking between them in long, greedy strokes. I dug my nails into his shoulders, feeling every ridge of his hot tongue—in exactly the right spots.

I squirmed, back arching as he lapped slowly, then faster, his mouth moving softly against my clit as I moaned and wailed in his grip. He started swirling his tongue, its odd texture shifting the sensation as I crooned wordlessly.

My hips rolled convulsively with each lash of his tongue, and I heard the same cry burst from my lips each time they did.

"Ah... ah... ah..."

I dug my heels into the padding and pushed myself upward against his face, feeling my whole body tighten, every muscle clenching at once.

"Don't stop," I begged, even knowing he couldn't understand me. "Don't stop!"

He didn't. And seconds later, I exploded.

I hissed and thrashed, the contractions setting loose bursts of ecstasy all through me. It was stronger than I had ever felt in my life, and even as it almost terrified me with its intensity, I wanted more.

The last contraction rocked through me; I collapsed to the floor, panting, already reaching for him in invitation. My tingling cunt might have calmed a little after climax, but I still had to have him inside me.

He crouched at my parted thighs, hesitating, his loincloth still confining him. I sat up drowsily and stroked my hand over his bulging groin. He froze. I untied the knots at his hips and freed him, his cock bounding up against his belly as he let out a grunt of relief.

I stared for a moment. He was big, all right, and his cock had ridges on it as well, subtle ones, except at the base where they stood up more prominently. It looked like one of those specialty dildos I had seen at the local sex shop.

I wonder how it will feel.

I smiled and lay back, holding out a hand to him. He had come to the end of his patience, and as he threw himself over me, I moaned with anticipation.

His cock slid in slowly and stopped, allowing my body to adjust to his huge girth. Then smoothly, he inched in some more, and the first ridge entered. The next one was just a bit wider, stretching me open a little farther. Each successive bump sent a jolt of hot pleasure through me. When he finally sank into me all the way, he drew out again, and I arched up on my heels as the ridges dragged against the sides of my tingling, aching cunt.

Holy fuck, that's good.

His head fell back, and a long, growling groan echoed around the space as he found a rhythm against me. He pushed firmly into me as he lifted my ass, his powerful thighs and belly flexing as he rolled his hips. He was big enough that it almost hurt, even so soon after climax, but I sure as hell didn't mind. Especially when his width set off aftershocks that left me gasping with fresh pleasure.

He started to thrust, his whole body taut with lust as he rolled his hips against me. Every movement of his cock pulled a groan from his throat as if he were so relieved to finally be fucking me that it was like a terrible pain was gone. I held him, as much to keep from being slid across the floor as to be close to him.

He moved slowly at first, his expression creasing with focus with every thrust. His breath rattled in his chest like he was carrying a boulder up a hill. As he moved against me, he shook so hard that I half expected he would burst any second. Instead, he continued pumping in and out, his hips slowly gathering speed as he growled low.

I lifted my hips to meet his as the unfamiliar texture of his cock intensified the pleasure coiling within my cunt. The thick base of his staff felt huge and hard as it pressed against me. I shimmied against his cock, making him grunt and thrust harder.

His hips began moving faster.

He kissed me fiercely and then shuddered and started moving at full speed. My body adjusted to the rhythm as lust raced through me, begging for more. His thrusts shook my whole body, and I hung on fiercely as my cunt tightened around him.

One pair of his hands held him up, the other roughly kneaded my ass as he lifted me against him. I wrapped my legs around his hips.

Seconds later, the pounding I was taking set my body off again. I let out a surprised cry as my pussy contracted around him even harder than before. The cave seemed to dissolve around me. I moaned into his mouth, and then, as my thrashing stopped, I went limp in his arms.

His conquest of my flesh seemed to drive him even wilder. He rumbled low in his throat and kept moving, the sharp slap of skin on skin rising above the pounding hiss of the rain outside. His back arched, his body poised above mine, every muscle taut, his skin gleaming with sweat, and his hair tangled into damp spikes.

For a moment—as he lingered on the edge, lips parted, eyes wide, and his body moving like a machine—it looked as if he were witnessing a miracle. He tensed and squeezed his eyes closed, then roared loud enough to rival the thunder outside.

His cock pulsed inside me, and I felt a rush of hot fluid that repeated in waves. He held me tight, panting and shuddering while his climax went on and on. It felt like his seed would start overflowing. But a moment later, his cock shuddered to a stop and so did he, deep relief and contentment on his face.

He barely managed to settle onto the padded floor without squishing me, instead rolling us over so I rested on his broad chest. There we lay, catching our breath.

"Ella," he murmured breathlessly. The wildfire in his eyes had banked to soft embers, and he smiled tenderly as he stroked my hair back from my face.

"Yes," I barely managed. I couldn't move much. I didn't want to either. Instead, I just kissed him under his chin and laid my head back down.

He chuckled gently and murmured something in his own language that I couldn't understand.

"What was that?" I mumbled sleepily.

A long silence. I was about to lift my head when I heard a faint snore.

Smiling, I closed my eyes.

CHAPTER 22
TEKEN

IF THE FIRST kiss stole my reason, the first climax brought it back... for a while. My Wulfaen side had come to the fore in our joining, very nearly starting the mating ritual. It had been all I could do to keep from flipping her over onto her stomach and pummeling her hot, gripping sex with a fiery friction that would push her into a fierce orgasm just as I sank my elongated fangs deep into the muscle where her throat met her shoulder—giving her the mating bite. As it was, I'd nearly nipped her sensitive throat at least once in my dominance.

When I woke from my slumber, I felt content, as if some missing piece of me had finally been returned. Ella's scent was all over me, and mine, as she lay in my arms, was all over her, a warning to all other males to keep their hands off the treasure that was mine alone—if they wanted to live.

The warm weight lying atop me stirred and sighed as I lifted my head and then settled back down.

I smiled. *Still fast asleep.*

It was nice to know I'd pleased my female, even though I had to proceed with caution so I wouldn't hurt my fragile human. I hadn't known for certain that I'd made the right decision to mate with her in what I assumed to be the human way until I had felt Ella's sex shudder and contract against my lips.

I had found my mate and pleased her. I knew from the way her body had reacted. And the sounds she had made—they were so gratifying.

My sheleki.

I felt a deep swell of pride at having pleased her enough that she now slept so deeply. I might not have put a pup in her belly yet, but now I knew I could coax her into approaching the effort with real enthusiasm.

I buried my face into my mate's neck, pulling her scent into my lungs. Her sweet fragrance tamed and calmed my Wulfaen, starting in my nostrils and winding its way through my body. Darting my tongue out, I tasted the skin along her throat, lapping reverently at her dark, soft flesh.

How I adored her, especially right now in this first quiet moment amid the mating frenzy. If anything, I was even more determined to get us back safely.

I rolled over to gently deposit her on the padded floor, got up, and walked outside, not bothering with my loincloth. Brax was watching, ears up as he peered out into the rainy darkness. I got us both some jerked meat and patted his ears as I offered him some.

Nude, I stood at the mouth of the cave, watching the water sluice past on its way into the jungle-clogged valley below. I filtered some for Brax and myself, then stepped out a little onto the ledge, letting the rainwater pour over my sweaty body. I tossed my head, sighing a little with relief as the itch went away. I only regretted that it took Ella's scent with it.

It was now raining so hard that the hoverbikes couldn't fly at all. I couldn't see their lights anywhere. They had either returned to base or were huddled in some dark, miserable camp somewhere in the jungle. *Good.* Either way, they wouldn't be able to see us or travel.

It was a stroke of luck. I was going to need more time with Ella. She was not yet marked, and that bothered my Gladiator and inner beast. Without Ella wearing my mating bite, another Gladiator could try to challenge my claim. Not likely—ever—but instincts were instincts.

In my current state, the sharp sting of rain on my tingling skin was enough to arouse me all over again. Soon, my thoughts would get blurry again, and the mating urge would take over.

As I held the drinking vessel for Brax, in the back of my head, I felt the briefest worry.

What if the storm lets up before I get full control of myself again? What if they catch us while I am helpless here?

I would fight like a wild beast to protect my mate while in the frenzy, but if caught mid-mating, we would both be vulnerable.

I had even tried to warn her, though our language barrier might have gotten in the way.

I would have wished that she had not kissed me until we reached my pack, but I felt too good about the results to worry much.

I filled the vessel a last time and brought it to Ella. She lay there half curled on her side, head on her arms, a faint, relaxed smile on her face. My heart swelled a little to see her that way—free, at ease, and happy in mating with me.

Once we got to my sector, I would present her to the elders and have our union acknowledged. We would have our whole lives to learn each other's ways and find joy together.

Now I just had to find a balance between my urge to consummate our bond and the need to get her to safety. *But how?*

In my bag, I had the suppressant spray I'd used to break her own mating frenzy, but that had been artificial. What Ella and I had was completely natural. The urges to mate would keep coming back until her scent changed and I knew my seed had taken. The suppressant wouldn't work as well on me; it would only lengthen the time between urges.

At least that's something we can resort to in an emergency.

I walked over and fished the spray from

Brax's saddlebags and glanced out at the rain before smiling and setting it on top of the bag. If I needed it, I would use it. But that wouldn't be for hours. And I wanted to take advantage of that extra time.

I returned to the enclosure and stepped inside, then stretched out beside Ella. She rolled toward me in her sleep, making a small, contented sound in her throat, and I stroked her hair, wondering a little at how strangely life could work out sometimes. I had come to that terrible place to start the process of rescuing all those kidnapped females and sending them home free. Instead, I had found my true mate, and I wanted to keep her forever.

And I'll kill any accursed slaver that gets in my way.

I nuzzled her hair, cuddling her close with two arms while the other two started exploring her skin. The frenzy burned low in my belly, rising slow and sweet, promising to overtake me soon. My cock was already throbbing. I paused, frowning slightly, and glanced over my shoulder at the rain.

Am I taking too much of a risk? Should I spray both of us?

Slowly, I turned my gaze back to Ella.

No. It will be fine. We have a little while yet before the storm stops.

Besides, it was too late. The mating frenzy was racing through my body. Struck by a wave of dizziness, I felt my staff ache, and I started kissing her neck.

She stirred again, and her dark, depthless eyes opened, looking up at me softly as I leaned over her. "Hey." She murmured the greeting, then some syllables I didn't recognize.

I had better things to do than talk—like take her several times. I leaned down to nibble at the corner of her mouth. She let out a soft croon and slid her hand up my back and through my hair. Little two arms had left some scratches on me last night, but the residual nanites in my system had cleaned those up completely while we slept.

I clambered over her and nuzzled against her back, brushing her hair aside and kissing her nape. My upper hands reached around to knead those lovely breasts. I couldn't get over their softness or their bounty. It delighted me to see how easily I could make her shiver and jump just by stroking her big, tender nipples.

My lower hands occupied themselves roaming over her hips, finding the little creases where her thighs met them, and kneading to make her squirm. I couldn't decide which sensations I liked best—the soft sensitivity of her breasts or the robust muscles of her ass.

Now that most of the barriers between us had melted away, she seemed to love being touched. Maybe my pheromones affected her more than I had thought, for she also seemed easier to warm up this time. Her nipples went tight quickly, her breath took on that little tremble I was learning to love, and her back arched, pressing her ass comfortably against me.

I noticed she could only handle so much teasing of her nipples before she started flinching slightly, and I had to switch to gentle stroking and kneading instead. But that gorgeous ass, those powerful thighs, I could really dig into, and all she did was purr.

It gave me... ideas.

My lower hands slipped around her hips again and ran themselves one at a time over her tight slit. Her short curls were already damp, so my fingers slid through them and parted her lips. She gasped, the sweet scent of her arousal reaching my nose.

My eyes widened, and the heat rising inside me suddenly rushed throughout my body. I heard myself let out a low growl, and I pushed up against her, my hard staff sliding between her squeezed-together thighs.

I thrust against her smooth skin slowly and reflexively as I slid a finger into her warm opening. My other hand busied itself stroking and kneading her pussy, careful not to apply too much pressure to that sensitive nub of flesh. Humans were a little different from a Gladiator female, but not by much. Mostly, they just needed gentler handling in certain spots. But I was happy to oblige, especially when small efforts yielded such huge results.

She thrashed slowly, rubbing her sex against the top of my shaft as I focused on pleasuring her for as long as I could stand. My head was throbbing with the need to mate. My cock ached for her even more than before, but I held out as long as I could, until she started to cry out with pleasure.

I caressed her through her climax until she went pleasantly limp. Then I let her go and rolled to my knees behind her. Taking her by the hips, I eased her onto her knees and pulled that gorgeous rump against my erection. She whimpered something that sounded encouraging, her breath still coming in long pants. And I couldn't wait anymore.

I fit the head of my cock into her and pushed in from behind, steadying her with two hands while I stroked her slit softly. She pushed back against me, hips bobbing intoxicatingly against my loins as I slid in deep. She cooed, forehead propped on her arms, and pushed back firmly.

I couldn't help but let out a long, sharp shout as she ground her ass against my shaft. I ran my hands up and down her back, gasping half-coherent endearments, my belly flexing as I moved slowly. Then I grabbed her ass firmly and started riding her in earnest.

She panted and whined as my hips began slapping against her ass hard, my cock sheathing itself in her firmly each time. Her soft walls clung to and slid over me, engulfing me in their hot embrace and quickly tightening around me. My fingers played more quickly against her womanhood, tugging at the hood, stroking, swirling, sometimes kneading the flesh around it firmly until she sobbed and bucked harder.

I pounded into her, more focused than ever on claiming her for good. All I had to do was thoroughly possess her and get us all home safely—and both were going to be work. But one was far more pleasant than the other.

I pounded against her, hips bouncing roughly while I felt my loins tightening toward climax. Our cries mixed, pushed out of us in time with our breath and the smack of our bodies. Her cunt contracted firmly around me and then rippled with spasms as she stretched beneath me and moaned.

Her writhing inflamed me further. I sped up my thrusts, drunk on lust and need. My pleasure mounted with each one, leaving me bounding eagerly after the next until I was blindly thrusting into her as fast as I could. She squealed somewhere during my madness. I felt her clench around me again and then collapse in my grip.

The sounds I made were those of a beast as I drove into her with wild excitement.

"Ella," I whispered. "Ella—"

I bent forward and covered her, sinking my elongated fangs, slick with serum, deep into the muscle where her throat met her shoulder and forever marking her as mine.

I almost roared my pleasure. My staff grew even larger inside her until the force of my volcanic release jetted against the mouth of her womb and pushed her into a violent spasm.

The haze lifted, and I discovered us curled together on our sides, my chest to her back as she whimpered sleepily and struggled to catch her breath. I smiled, licked my bite mark to heal her, then kissed the back of her neck before settling in behind her.

Licking her blood from my fangs, I gave another glance at the cave mouth. Brax was still on duty, and I was too sated and sleepy to worry about anything.

CHAPTER 23

ELLA

"ELLA, SWEETHEART?"

Mom and I were drinking tea on the porch of her home. It was mid-spring, and a cardinal was singing its lyrical song from the bushes.

I looked over at her and smiled a little awkwardly. "Yeah, Mom?"

"You, uh, want to tell me why your new boyfriend is a four-armed alien? Grandma and Grandpa are asking a lot of questions."

"Oh. Uh... that. Well, there's a really crazy story behind that, Mom..."

I woke up slowly, sore, sticky, but more relaxed than I'd ever been in my life. A faint bluish glow, like moonlight, sparkled through my eyelashes as my eyelids fluttered. For long moments, I had no idea where I was. Not in my bed at my apartment. Not in my room at my mom's. Not in the cage.

So where the fuck…?

Beside me, a large, warm shape rolled over and draped two muscular arms over me. I heard a soft grunt and a sigh.

Oh.

I opened an eye to Teken's sleeping face, the enclosure beyond, and the enormous mound of fur curled up on its far side. Brax looked up at his master's movements and thumped his tail.

"Hey, pup," I mumbled softly.

He lolled his tongue hello, wagged his tail again, and then laid his head on his paws.

I stretched carefully in Teken's grip, amazed at how well-rested I felt.

How long had it been, sleeping fitfully in that too-small cage, wary of anyone approaching while I slept? Long enough that I had developed a dull, lingering headache and hadn't noticed it until now, when I felt relief.

I ran my hands over myself, doing a quick inventory. Teken had gone more than a little wild on me. I had a few sore spots that felt like they were going to turn into either suck marks or bruises. Tiny ones on my back and ass, larger on my neck and breasts and the upper insides of my thighs. My pussy was fine, despite taking one hell of a pounding.

The discovery of all those spots, evidence of what we had been doing for hours, turned me on again. Even that freaky animal biting thing he did to my shoulder triggered a sharp climax that had me pulsing around him so hard that I nearly screamed at the top of my lungs from the sheer ecstasy.

I had no clue I was into getting bitten by an alien while he pummeled my cunt like a recently released prisoner.

My nipples tightened, and a sharp tingle ran up my lower back. My body felt renewed, and in every movement, the resonance of his physical possession echoed within me.

This is all so weird... in a good way. How could I ever have imagined that the man for me, the one who would really have my number in the sack, would be a four-armed alien from a world I had been kidnapped to? How the hell could I ever explain this to Mom?

Mom... I blushed reflexively.

This was not the time nor the place to be thinking about her approval. Not when I was still butt naked and thinking about riding Teken's talented, huge alien cock again.

It's weird as hell how things worked out. Aside from the whole running for our lives part and the whole fucked-up way we met, well... I really think I could do worse.

But I still wonder if he's the kind of guy—I mean alien—I could bring home to Mom. Even discounting the "the neighbors would call the National Guard" issue.

I wanted to go home. I had people I cared about there.

The problem was I was starting to care about Teken.

How am I going to find a compromise that will let me keep my connections on Earth and with him?

I sighed. *Survive first. Worry about your love life second.*

Wait, did I say love life? Shit. Well, it looks like I got attached to the alien.

I slipped free of the double circle of his arms and got up to stretch. My joints and muscles popped, and I ached a little in unfamiliar places.

Being with Teken was the best sex of my life. And just that thought had me shook. *I need to keep my head together.*

Brax yawned hugely and leaned into a good head scratch, then settled back down to sleep. His fur was damp, and he seemed tired.

He was guarding us all night, poor, loyal thing. And I'm damn glad of it.

It was still raining and thundering loudly, but the earlier monsoon had lessened to a downpour. Dawn had broken outside, flooding the cave with thin light. I drained the water bottle, then moved to the cave mouth to refill it and rinse off in the rain. The weird calls of unfamiliar creatures were starting to rise from the jungle as the storm slowly began to dry up.

Then I heard what I swore was the hoot of a nearby owl, and I blinked. I looked back at the dog again, sleeping soundly. *More imports from Earth?*

I enjoyed the earthy scent of Teken's body on my skin, but the itchiness of dried sweat got to be too distracting after a while. The rain was still warm enough to be comfortable, despite the early-morning hours. I wondered just how hot it got here.

I know so little about this planet.

I didn't know if the slavers were outlaws or accepted by this society. And I was still perplexed about where Teken stood on the subject of his people buying hostesses from the Omers. He seemed to dislike the whole slave thing, but according to what I learned at the facility, his people needed females to mate with or his race would go extinct.

Is that all I am to him—a birthing vessel?

No. That's a ridiculous theory. No one in their right mind would risk their life over a potential baby mama. There had to be more to Teken's story.

Is he some sort of cop? A vigilante?

I paused, a brief chill washing over me.

A competitor? Is he just kidnapping me and seducing me so he can pimp me out later?

The shock of suspicion ran through me and away so fast that it barely made an impression.

No, that's silly. He wouldn't have treated me so kindly and protectively if all that were true. But my immediate reaction did point out just how little I knew about my new lover, aside from his devotion to me.

Maybe someone hired him to rescue me.

No. That doesn't make sense. Who would hire him?

Mom didn't know any aliens. I was pretty sure she would have mentioned that shit, given she was crappy at keeping secrets. And she was the only one I could think of who would be willing to pay a ransom for me.

She must be so worried. I must get back to her or let her know that I'm okay somehow. Teken will help me. He must—once he sees how important this is to me. Right?

I finished rinsing out my hair and combing my fingers through the thickness as I stared out over the jungle. The rain was now down to a misty drizzle. I stepped back, wringing my hair out, and let myself dry while I pondered my next moves.

The warm air brushed against my skin as it rose from the jungle, scented heavily with flowers, greenery, and mud. Now and again, the musk of some animal slipped past my nostrils.

It's beautiful. Especially after Teken left me feeling this good. But it's still hard to enjoy it while I'm scared for my life.

I had to trust that my new companion had my best interests in mind. He certainly acted that way, but because I couldn't talk things out with him, I had no idea how to ask about his motives. And why did he think I was his mate?

I wanted to know where we were going and how long it would take to get there. And interrogate him about important things like who he worked for and what would happen once we reached our destination.

It was like walking around blindfolded and trusting a stranger to guide me unharmed. But at least Teken was working hard for my trust and not just expecting it.

Oh, and there was the fact that he was amazing when it came to sex. Which made me wonder why he was so skilled and tireless. *Is that a Wulfaen Gladiator "I can go all night long" thing?*

The expression on his face was like I was his new drug, which was more than a little flattering, giving me a strange rush of pussy power. But I'd never been a manipulative woman, and I preferred to deal with people directly and honestly, especially men.

Shit. Some men found my honesty off-putting. Many found it refreshing—once they realized it was genuine. But right now, looking back over my shoulder at my sleeping alien, I wondered, *How much would he do for me if I wanted him to?*

I lifted an eyebrow. He was an amazing lover, a brave warrior, and a devoted guard, and he couldn't get enough of me—and I him. And weirdly enough, he was a better listener than most guys I had been with, even though Teken and I only shared knowledge of a few dozen words.

I'm really tempted to try to find a way to take him back to Earth with me, which is a ridiculous idea. He wouldn't fit on Earth, and I have no idea if it would be safe to bring Mom here.

I stiffened when the reality of my situation sank in.

What if I can't go back home? Could I be happy on this planet with Teken?

Frankly, I didn't know.

I loved my mom and the life I had on Earth, but there was a real possibility that I would never be able to return. And sooner rather than later, I'd have to figure out what my new life would be like on this alien world.

Turning back toward the jungle view, I spotted six hoverbikes rising above the tree line. A few of them were pointed in my direction.

Shit! I ducked back out of sight, very aware that I was naked and, worse, unarmed. My clothes were back in the tent. But hadn't Teken been wearing a strange-looking pistol on his hip before he had stripped down to tend his wounds? His belt was in the saddlebags with his now-mended clothes. Well out of my reach.

"Teken!" I called in a panic. "Teken, wake up!"

He barely stirred, but then Brax popped his head up and his ears lifted. The dog let out a thunderous growl, and Teken sat up at once.

I started digging frantically through the saddlebags, looking for the damn gun, while the sound of one of the hover engines drew steadily closer.

CHAPTER 24

TEKEN

ELLA'S frightened voice cut through my post-mating slumber. I was already waking when Brax's warning growl brought me to full alertness. I sat up and opened my eyes, taking in the scene.

Ella, still gorgeously naked but now tense with fear, was digging through my saddlebags with an air of desperation. Worse, I could hear a hover engine approaching.

I immediately cut the lights of the tent and grabbed Brax's collar, signaling for him to go silent. Ella was at least staying quiet, but she kept moving around closer to the cave entrance as she struggled to find something. As the sound grew nearer, however, she had the sense to duck down.

A dark shape briefly blocked most of the light at the entrance. I braced myself, trying to ignore the first stirrings of fresh lust at the base of my spine. My sheleki was endangered, and protecting her was my only focus right now.

After a moment, two more shadows paused in the cave mouth, then swept on again, their engines humming. I leaped to my feet as soon as they were gone, intent on joining Ella. I couldn't call out to her and instruct her to come to me without alerting the catcher. I would have to go to her.

Brax trembled with excitement but stayed obediently where he was as I rose and moved along the wall toward Ella. She pulled out my swords and laid them aside for me, then kept digging, being as stealthy and quick to duck down as she could.

I edged along the wall toward her, back to the stone, ready to dip behind one of the outcrops if another slaver paused at the entrance. I wanted to shift into my Wulfaen, but the energy it would take to morph into my beast— swiftly killing the intruders before the rest of the catchers arrived—could jeopardize my ability to protect my mate. This was a risk I wasn't yet willing to take.

Ella looked up as I came toward her and smiled with relief. But the brief distraction of our eyes meeting nearly proved fatal. Brax suddenly growled again, and another shadow appeared in the doorway before Ella could get behind the cover of our gear.

The hoverbike landed in the flat, dry spot just beyond the entryway, blasting us with air from its fans. Two figures jumped off—and I heard them talking as the engine cycled down.

"These caves are full of shovel-claws. No one would stay here." The first one was smaller and younger-sounding than the other, but I couldn't see features. Only dark silhouettes against the bright cave mouth.

"That alien had a riding dog. They eat shovel-claws for breakfast. Those things run at the smell of dogs every damn time. We have to check every cave, or Belland will find out for sure." Dazzled by daylight, they did not yet see us as they dismounted. "I'm more scared of him than a hundred shovel-claws."

"You have a point. Let's search this section using the climbing ropes and report back. I need my teaberry broth, or I'm not ever going to wake up fully." A sigh and shuffling from the younger one. "Where's my damn wrist lamp?"

"It's supposed to be on your wrist, youngling." The elder sounded so tired that I almost felt sorry for him. I was still going to take off his head, though.

"Well, it's broad daylight. I must have left it back at camp."

The brewing argument distracted them as I snuck the last few body lengths.

I made it to Ella's side and grabbed my swords just as the elder's wrist lamp speared through the darkness, illuminating a very naked Ella from the waist up. She froze with a squeak that was half terror and half embarrassment.

Both catchers stopped and stared for a moment, wide-eyed and slack-jawed. It would have been almost comical if it weren't for the fact that the bosom they were so captivated by was attached to my female.

She ducked out of sight, and the older one laughed. "Hey, pretty earthling, don't be scared now. We're here to bring you back alive."

"You think he ran off and left her?" the younger one breathed, drawing a bit nearer as Ella swore and dug deep into the second saddlebag. I tensed as I crouched beside her just out of sight, my blades held in my upper hands.

"Seems fair. I figure he's not a noble at all, just some thief that gave up when we came after him in force. Go grab her."

Brax let out a low warning growl as the younger one, face a blur in the dimness, reached out for Ella's shoulder. Immediately, the beam and both males turned toward Brax's hulking shape in the darkness. I leaped silently from my hiding place and attacked.

The younger male screamed as my blade bit deep into his shoulder and then went silent as the other sent his head spinning out of the cave mouth. I dove for the elder and then ducked aside quickly as he opened fire on me.

Brax lunged forward, only to be driven back by gunfire himself. I tried to lunge while the veteran catcher was occupied with my dog, but he was too canny and fast. I ended up diving again. My inner beast pressed against my skin, fighting to come out and rip apart this male, but I shoved him down. It was my Gladiator's time to protect my female, and I'd trained for years to do so.

"You'd best give yourselves up now before Belland gets here! He'll notice we're gone soon enough. You'll much prefer how you'll be treated if you come quietly." He glanced over at Ella as he held us at bay and frowned slightly when he noticed she had ducked out of sight. "Eh? Where'd you go, female?"

"She can't understand you," I snapped as I feinted a lunge, and Brax growled louder.

"Doesn't matter. You can hear me well enough. Get the little earthling to come out, and I'll let you all live." He took a long step toward the pile of gear, his smirk widening. "Especially if she keeps her top off."

Ella popped up suddenly, glorious breasts and all, a grim look on her face that, from the delighted look on the catcher's face, he'd missed completely. She lifted my energy pistol in a good two-handed grip and started firing. The sharp cracks of the pistol were accompanied only by a bluish glow at the end of the muzzle. The first shot killed him, but she didn't stop firing until he slumped to the ground.

Ella stood frozen, panting hard, still holding the weapon on the dead slaver until I reached her, gently pressing down on her arms to lower her gun. She glanced up at me uncertainly.

My little female was a fierce human Gladiator. She would do well ruling by my side as the alpha female of my pack.

"We go," I managed in her language and gestured at our gear.

She nodded and offered me the pistol.

Smiling, I shook my head and handed her the gun belt. It was my duty to protect my mate, but if she was that good a shot under pressure, it was time to provide her the means to defend herself.

We both dressed, and then I approached the two corpses, which lay in their own mess near the cave mouth. I knew we couldn't steal the hoverbike and escape. If this Belland had any brains, he would have trackers installed in the thing, which meant we had to get rid of it quickly. Both slavers had energy pistols, but the weapons were a lower capacity than my own. I decided to leave Ella with mine, and I strapped both of theirs to my hips just in front of my knife sheaths. Grabbing the older slaver's communicator off his ear, I turned off the speaking volume, then put it on listening mode.

"Continue searching the caves until they are all done. Move along the range and check each one on foot." I recognized the voice as Belland's.

Suddenly, muffled screaming erupted over the communicator. *"Sir!"* One of the men gasped. *"We've disturbed a pack of shovel-claws! They got Eirlan!"*

Belland let out an exasperated sigh. *"Unit three, reinforce unit four at their position. If they're dead when you get there, throw in a gas bomb and move on."*

Hurriedly, I strapped on Brax's riding pad and saddlebags, then went back to deflate the enclosure into its shell. Scooping up the arm-wide disk that was left, I shoved it into the top of one bag, then strapped everything down.

"Ella," I said sharply, and I heard her mutter something as she hurried over.

I helped her onto Brax and then turned to the hoverbike. There was only one way to make sure the slavers weren't drawn here before we could slip away, and that was to use their mode of transportation as a distraction.

Ella exclaimed something in shock and disgust as I grabbed both bodies and put them on the hoverbike, tying them into their saddles. Starting the engine, I checked the location of the other bikes on the view screen and then engaged the autopilot.

I leaped onto Brax's back, grabbing his harness grips with two hands while holding on to my mate with the other two. The hoverbike rose, its engines blowing dust all over the cavern, and then hummed forward into the light, rising and picking up speed.

Belland noticed at once and spoke loudly over the communicators. *"Unit two, you are off course. Repeat, why are you idiots leaving the search site? Unit two, respond!"*

Nothing but crackling quiet. *"Units one and five, break off and intercept unit two. Their bike seems to be malfunctioning. Or maybe it's the damn pilots."* Belland sounded ready to rip someone's head clear off.

I grinned as I spoke to Brax. "Go on, boy."

Brax sprang out of the cave mouth and scrambled down the slope into the trees as two hoverbikes peeled off from the cliffside to chase after their runaway unit. I heard the whine of their engines intensify as the autopilot sped the two-man bike to its limit.

We made it into the cover of the trees by the time the dead catchers' hoverbike reached the far end of its looping path and swung back around toward the caves. I could hear slavers yelling and cursing on the communicators and someone still screaming faintly. Shovel-claw snarls echoed from somewhere, and over it all, Belland's raspy voice rained down every curse I knew and a few I did not.

Ella craned her neck to try to spy the course of the vehicles above the tree line, but it was pointless. I could still listen in on the fun, however.

"Teams still at the caves, update."

"They're eating us!" a slaver shrilled, followed by screaming.

Belland let out a low, exasperated growl. *"Unit two, is your communicator functioning? Unit two, cut your speed. You're heading into the cliffs too fast!"*

"Sir! They're headed straight for the cave with units three and four!" This slaver sounded even younger than the one I had beheaded and very panicked.

"*Shoot them down!*" Belland roared at once. "*Shoot them—*"

An impact and explosion rocked the ground slightly and filled the communication line with overloud static. Belland's furious cursing could barely be heard underneath.

I laughed, coaxing Brax back on the long run toward home.

CHAPTER 25

ELLA

MY MIND WAS a jumble of thoughts as we raced away.

I just killed someone.

I knew what these men were after—returning me to their compound to be caged, drugged, pawed at, fucked, and sold. It was them or me, and I did the right thing in defending myself and my alien lover.

But I still didn't know how I felt about the fact that I'd taken a life so easily or the fact that Teken had entrusted me with his terrifyingly powerful sidearm. He'd seemed almost proud of me. I guessed that made sense. After all, he was a Gladiator, and from the way he fought, he seemed to be trained in the act of deadly combat. Or maybe it turned him on that I was a little badass.

Did female Gladiators exist? And if so, did they fight alongside the men?

Based on everything I'd learned at the compound, I knew his people no longer had females—which made me sad that a race had lost all their women. But I had so many questions about the culture of the Wulfaen.

Were women equal in power to men? Or were they relegated to staying at home, taking care of their families?

When mud sprayed against my skin, I switched back to the matter at hand. Back in the cave, I'd been very lucky in at least three different ways. I'd spent some time at the firing range at home, so I knew my way around a standard Earth pistol. But that didn't help too much with alien technology. My second stroke of luck had turned out to be that the design of the weapon was surprisingly simple. Finally, that dumb slaver had been too busy staring at my big breasts to notice when I brought up the gun. Killing had never been something I thought I could do. But drastic circumstances called for drastic measures. And it was about survival for me and Teken.

Living in New York City, I had learned to defend myself as a matter of course, though I only had access to a firearm out in the country at my mom's house. She was an old army brat and took me shooting to relax now and again.

Mom always said you can't hesitate when your life is on the line.

I knew it was true and that she would be telling me this herself if she were here. But the aftermath of my first shooting still left me lightheaded and a little numb. What had happened almost didn't seem real. But then again, I could say that about many things that had happened to me lately. I focused on hanging on, praying we got away cleanly before anyone noticed us.

We rode through the dim jungle while the leaves dripped on us, and Brax's enormous paws pattered through the mud and several shallow streams. It was warming up more, the air starting to feel steamy, and I was suddenly glad I wasn't running under my own power. I was athletic, but in this heat, with those machines after us, I would have slowed everyone down.

I could hear the faint crackle of voices from the elaborate-looking earpiece Teken had stolen off the slaver I killed. He was listening in to hear where they were and what they were doing.

Good. Smart. It gives us more of a chance of making it out of this shit in one piece.

It also left me wondering again about his occupation. Right now, he was coming off a lot like a muscle-bound extraterrestrial James Bond, all cleverly improvised plans, good sex, and occasional extravagant violence.

He even managed some explosions. The thought made me chuckle a little, despite my lingering shock.

Maybe I should stop condemning myself for using lethal force when it was warranted. On the other hand, maybe it's good that I'm not completely comfortable with killing. It would be a lot more problematic if I were nonchalant about my actions.

We ran on for hours without hearing any engines. Teken kept listening intently to the earpiece as he guided us along, but from what I could tell, it got quieter. Maybe we were reaching the edge of their range, which would mean we really had left them behind, at least for a while.

I was even more impressed with him now,

and I knew I would have a hell of a time leaving him behind when we finally had a chance to talk this over with the help of a translator. I wanted to learn more of his language, but right now, this slow exchange of words and phrases couldn't help us all that much. It would take weeks for us to really start to understand each other, and we probably didn't have that much time before I headed back to Earth.

We journeyed on for at least an hour more before I started to notice something—Teken's grip on me was shifting. His breathing was growing unsteady and labored, with that little shake in it I remembered so well from last night. He was getting turned on again.

I confirmed it a moment later when Brax leaped over a broader stream and the landing jostled my ass against Teken's bulging groin. He groaned as though I had punched him in the gut, and his lower hands started to caress me through my clothes.

"Teken?" I asked anxiously, looking back at him over my shoulder.

His eyes were dilating again.

I stared into them, at that hazy look of mixed lust and growing concern, and I started to worry. *Oh shit. It's happening again, and this time, we don't have a safe hideout.*

"Ella," he groaned, and I tried to ignore the answering tingle in my cunt from his desperate tone. He managed a few understandable words in English. "Must stop..."

I reached back and gave his package a gentle squeeze and pat, nodding. *Poor guy. I need to figure out a way to get him off good and hard so we can take off again, or he's not going to make it much longer.*

I couldn't imagine what this must be like for him—completely obsessed with fucking me, the desire rising in cycles inside him and demanding satisfaction before he could function again.

Is his desperate need to have me a Wulfaen thing? Or does he have a high libido like me?

There was one thing that couldn't be denied—sex with Teken had been freaking fantastic. It was hands down the best climax I'd ever had, even with a vibrator. So truth be told, I wouldn't mind going another hot and sweaty round with my sexy alien. But we were on the run, and we didn't have time to deal with his demanding boner.

The spot where he bit me suddenly tingled. Reaching up, I scratched the skin, which was now completely scabbed over.

I frowned. *How could the bite heal so fast? And what is the deal with him biting me? Is it Gladiator foreplay?*

I remembered how deeply his teeth had sunk into my flesh. *Shit.* The shock of pain had been so excruciating that I'd nearly passed out. And then out of nowhere, a quick balm of relief had raced through my veins, almost as if I'd taken a pain reliever.

Most puzzling... *Why did I enjoy him marking me in such a primitive way?*

Everything about being with Teken was strange and, yes, exciting. He was an alien that shifted into a wolf, and instead of being afraid of his dual sides, I was intrigued and wanted to know everything about him. And then there were the feelings I was starting to develop.

I liked him more than I should, given that our relationship was only temporary. But no matter how hard I tried to keep my emotions in check, I couldn't, and I sensed he couldn't either. Our connection was deepening, and we didn't even speak the same damn language.

When we slowed down, my thoughts snapped back to the present. I heard him panting and groaning as he steered us toward an enormous tree on slightly higher ground. Finally, he halted Brax for a rest right beside two of its thick, overarching roots.

I managed to get down by myself, but I immediately had to stretch my aching back and legs. Between last night's exercise and this morning's long ride, I was stiff and sore as hell. But this shit still beat the damn cage by a lot.

Grabbing Brax some jerky from the saddlebags, I then turned to look at Teken, who was leaning against the tree, eyes closed, struggling to catch his breath. Little groans escaped his parted lips as he clutched at the bark with all four hands.

Smiling, I walked over to him, pressing my body up against him familiarly. He opened his eyes and gave me a look of drunken, lusty desperation as his hands reached to stroke over my hair and back.

"Ella," he mumbled, and then he said a few rolling words in his language that I hadn't heard before.

I put a hand on his chest and smiled at

him reassuringly. "Don't worry. I'll take care of you."

His brows drew together in confusion, but I was already reaching for the lacing on the front of his codpiece. His eyes widened and then slid closed as a faint smile replaced the look of agony on his face.

His cock sprang loose as soon as I unlaced his codpiece fully, and he let out a soft grunt of relief. He moaned as I took his silky-skinned, heavily ridged organ between my hands and started exploring every inch of it with my fingertips. I shivered as I touched his hardness. He was long and beautifully thick. He gasped at the teasing, his back arching slightly, and thrust his cock slowly into my hands as I caressed it.

I stroked him gently. "Damn," I whispered.

He was the epitome of fucking masculine perfection. His engorged, thick manhood stretched taut, almost past his navel. The thick, round crown glistened with a small drop of moisture. His balls were tight with arousal.

My cunt tingled, and my peaks puckered as I craved the salty taste of him. Aggressively,

I grabbed his manhood with both hands, feeling the hardness swell. Massaging the smooth, hot column of flesh between my fingers, I slid to my knees, then leaned forward to take the swollen head into my greedy mouth.

He went rigid, his low, rhythmic cries taking on a shocked note. I looked up at him, smiling mischievously around his shaft, and saw him staring down at me in amazement.

What? Don't alien females suck cock? Well... let me show you a thing or two.

Feathering my tongue over him, swirling the salty pre-come from the tip of his crown, I savored his earthy taste. Cupping his balls, I rolled my fingers over his tight sack. My other hand firmly gripping him, I explored the peaked ridge just under the head of his shaft with my tongue.

He stretched upward, chest heaving, muscles going taut as he panted. He submitted himself totally to what I was doing, not touching me, not daring to move.

I embraced his length with both hands before my lips greedily slid over the head of his arousal. Teken's hands threaded through my hair as though savoring the feel of it.

The low groans coming from him spurred me on.

He grew bigger in my mouth as I bobbed my head up and down over his wide shaft. The more I tasted, the more I hungered. With every flick of my tongue, the hard grip of his fingers against my head seemed to turn me on even more. I fed him into my throat, taking it all. His hard shaft was thick and broad, like him. My lips stretched around his man flesh. He spread his legs wider.

I hummed as he started a slow slide in and out between my lips. A fog of desire clouded my vision. All I could think of was bringing him pleasure. His groan deepened, becoming more of a growl, charging the erotic tension even more.

My body quivered with a fire I'd never felt before. My tongue stroked every bump and ridge of his flesh. Moving up and down on him, I sucked him harder. I was thrilled when his little exclamations went longer, hoarser. I sped up, adding more pressure gradually. He writhed against the tree, his fingertips cracking bark as he clutched at it. His cock started throbbing harder.

He tightened his fists even more in my

hair. My mouth opened wider, and he inched his staff until he was lodged against the back of my throat. He was huge, the size of my wrist, but I didn't back away or struggle.

Holding still, I relaxed my throat to keep from gagging. My tongue slid along his length as I breathed through my nose. He said something in his language, his voice hoarse and thick with arousal.

Heady with power, I swallowed around him. The sound of his harsh breathing drove me on as he thrust into me with a slow rhythm that was rough and primal.

Fingers tangled in my hair, he held my head still for his deep thrusts. My lips danced over him. My hips swayed in tandem.

"Sheleki," he whispered. He was squirming and trembling against the tree, totally under my control, his voice strained with pleasure and growing distress as his balls drew up tight against his shaft.

Moisture pooled between my legs.

All too soon, a guttural groan erupted from his carnal mouth. He shot into the sweet depths of my mouth. I continued to suck, swallow, and lick him with gentle strokes until he gradually softened in my mouth.

After inching from between my lips with a heartfelt sigh, in one smooth motion, he helped me stand. My legs were trembling under me, and he cradled me against his chest with unexpected tenderness that left me speechless.

Gently, I pulled away from him, tucking his cock back into his clothes and lacing him up. I smiled up at him as he stared down at me, panting, his eyes still full of amazement.

"Ella," he whispered reverently. "My sheleki."

"Your freaky sheleki." I flashed him a naughty smile and winked, then jerked my head toward Brax. "Let's get back on the road."

CHAPTER 26

TEKEN

WHAT IN THE name of all the gods was that? Is taking a male into your mouth a human mating ritual?

None of the teachings about mating with a female Gladiator documented such an exciting and fulfilling sexual act. Perhaps it was because our mating practices focused on fertility, sometimes at the expense of other pleasures.

Apparently, humans had the opposite problem—they were too fertile. Maybe that was one of the reasons the gods had selected earthlings to be our compatible mating species. I supposed it made sense that lovers who did not seek pregnancy would please each other in other ways, but I had no idea being taken inside my sheleki's warm mouth could feel so incredible. I barely had strength left in my legs to climb into my saddle.

She was asking how I was in her strange, chirpy language, a nervous little laugh in her voice as she hovered close to me.

I managed to mumble, "Um, okay," and hoped that was right. But I still had a little difficulty pulling her up into the saddle in front of me.

As we settled in, I drew a deep breath of her sweet scent that was now intermingled with mine. Both Gladiator and Wulfaen were satisfied that all Wulfaen that dared to approach my female would know she had been claimed.

The mating urge had died back down to warm embers in the pit of my stomach. I would be all right for a while. Maybe not long enough to make the run to my sector, but I was going to do my best. The idea that the slave catchers might snag us during mating made me sick with rage. I would not allow that to happen, even if I had to soak myself in an icy river to reduce my cravings for Ella.

Gods, give me strength until we are safe and alone again. I don't want to take her on the ground of the council chamber as I give my report either.

We rode for our lives, as fast and straight as we dared toward my pack and the shelter of my sector. I knew in my heart that if we kept going without complications, my mate and I could spend the rest of our lives together. Now, if only I could make certain that's what she wanted.

I was not proud that I'd succumbed and marked her without explaining the seriousness of giving her the mating bite. According to our history, once a male marked his mate, the bite would not only bring pleasure to us both. It would make Ella stronger, and her eyesight and stamina would become better.

I must make absolutely certain she has a working translator. Rudimentary knowledge of each other's language won't give me the depth I need to tell her everything I'm feeling. I am devoted to her in every way. But I also know she was brought here against her will.

What if she wants to leave? What if she doesn't want to be with me forever?

She's beautiful and must have her choice

of males back on Earth. And though she desires me, can I measure up to one of her earthling males? They know her language and culture better than I ever could.

She's an amazing female from a planet I know so little about, aside from their genetic riches and the beauty of their females. How could I ever compete with a male of her nation? A male who comes to her offering everything I cannot?

My grip on her tightened slightly as we rode. She seemed to sense something was wrong because she stroked her right hand up and down my forearm, gently, reassuringly.

How will I find the right words, even with the aid of a translator, to tell her how I feel? And what would I give up to be by her side?

How do I tell her what becoming her mate has done for me? To me? I will never crave another female and will join the ranks of the old widowers if she goes back to Earth.

But how do I explain all of this—and everything else?

I had a lot to worry about once she finally got her translator and I, no doubt, had to answer her endless questions. I knew she had been brought here by force, and learning that the slavers were here operating legally and that they sold females to others for pleasure— including trying to sell earthlings to my people for mating—made me worry she would hate my world, its culture, and all of my Gladiator brethren for being so desperate that they wanted to do business with the Omers in hope of saving our race from extinction. But slavery was slavery, and that was not an act that I'd stand idly by and accept in my pack or any other.

But will she believe my stance against slavery? Or will she be so broken from her ill-treatment on my planet that she'd rather flee to Earth?

If that happened, it would break my heart to see her go, but her happiness and what she desired was my first and only priority.

Ella patted my hand again as she chatted enthusiastically about something I didn't understand. I longed to tell her that just her mere presence filled me with joy. She was unlike any female I'd ever met. Her body and mine had communed on a level I'd never experienced, and even though we had only scraps of language in common, we understood each other in a meaningful way.

I could already tell, by watching her expressions and gestures and the language of her body, the basic meaning behind any words she spoke. As I learned to pick out specific words and confirmed them with her, I also tried to sort out how they were used together. Humans seemed fond of long, complicated sentences. Or maybe that was just Ella.

Right now, as we traveled, she was saying something about the road ahead. "Where" asked for a direction or location. "City" was a gathering place. The best I could manage in her language was "Battle City"—my sector. Close enough for now, and she nodded as I pointed straight ahead.

My sector had scouted half a day's ride from the center of where the majority of my pack lived, watching the perimeter. They would radio in if the slavers got too close and would come out in force to resist any penetration of our airspace.

"Battle City... help us. We go."

Maybe I should have been looking forward to having a translator unit for her instead of dreading it slightly. I could only have faith that she would be patient when the time came for me to explain.

The slavers could not legally pursue her to the limits of my sector, but slavers rarely paid attention to that, especially since they thought they were above Gladiator law.

The Omers had vast wealth and many females that most races, including mine, needed for survival and, yes, pleasure. Slavers selling alien females wasn't new, but the earthling additions as hostesses were. Slavery was the shame of our nation—a planet ravaged by war and alien genetic weapons, altered by infertility and gender imbalance, and left distraught enough that many races would sacrifice their own honor and morals to bypass extinction. It was not in our nature as Gladiators to ever completely neglect our honor, so it angered me that some of the council had voted to buy hostesses to calm the needs of their pack, forgetting that their hopes to find their one true mate lay in the terror and violation of those very females they would one day claim to love.

But thinking about this dilemma only distracted me.

I need to focus.

In truth, I couldn't fully, not with my head clouded with this unfamiliar, creeping dread. I would have gladly fought every one of the slavers alone, for her sake, but at least I had experience in that kind of long odds.

Ella could slay me with a few cold words.

I had to concentrate on getting us back safely. I could ask her if she could be happy here later, when we didn't have a team of soulless, half-mechanical mercenaries hunting us.

I just wished I could get it out of my head for more than a minute at a time. But I disciplined myself and looked ahead, steering us around a nest of tentacle vines trailing, deceptively relaxed, across the path ahead.

Whatever else happens, no matter how much I must bleed to get you home safe, Ella, I will do so. And I will take pride in the fact that I did not buy my mate. But rather, I set her free.

I only pray she will spend her freedom at my side.

A few hours into our trek toward my sector, another downpour struck. This time, it was lighter, but it still cut visibility and sent winds whipping down through the leaves. We heard another crash just minutes later, and it was alarmingly close.

They're catching up to us, despite the storm. The cyborg must be pushing them recklessly. Some won't make it, but the rest are out here looking. If they overtake us, we may run into them when it clears up and be unable to get past them as easily.

And then there was the matter of the broadcasts I had listened in on earlier. Belland had sent more catchers to try to head off any escape to neighboring outposts that fell outside Gladiator control. I knew that included the perimeter of my sector, which meant if the blockade was too tight, we would have to go around or send a message through. Possibly both.

"Ella," I said as we hung on to the bounding dog. "Bad men ahead. Maybe many bad men."

She tried to answer in my language. "Machine man?"

Good, she remembered the cyborg, with his covered face and horrific, misshapen arm. "Yes."

She nodded and shivered, and I held her with my lower arms as I focused on the path ahead.

Brax caught a whiff of something ahead that he didn't like and slowed down, a low growl rumbling in his throat.

Coaxing him to stop in a nest of brush, I dismounted. "Stay. I check."

This strange Earth language had some unusual words, but Ella nodded, watching me wide-eyed as I walked away. She didn't try to follow.

There was a narrow valley up ahead that was filled with grassy meadowlands. We were still at least an hour's ride from the edge of pack lands and would have to cross it to take the most direct route. If my instincts were correct, it was the most logical place to expect an ambush, and Brax's growling had only made me more certain.

I moved to the edge of the tree line at the top of the ridge and looked down at a straggling line of hoverbikes hanging low over the valley floor.

Curse it. There are too many to try sneaking us through their line.

I withdrew slightly, burning with anger

and frustration, but not all that surprised. Looking along the ridge, I noticed where it joined with the slope of a gentler hill farther on, it was so densely covered with brush that life sensors would not be able to penetrate it.

I could hide there with Ella while Brax goes without his gear back to the sector with our message. Without his saddle and tack, he'll look like yet another feral beast. They're all over this region.

I had thought this plan a bit mad when I had first come up with it, but now, forced to put it into action, I couldn't afford to think that way. I had to believe it would work, even as I prepared for the worst.

Ella sighed with relief when she saw me. "Bad men?" she asked in her language.

"Yes." I pointed down the ridge toward the wooded slope, then hopped onto Brax. "We go."

Now, instead of running, I had to keep Brax down to a rapid walk. He panted and whined impatiently now and again, and I gently but firmly got him to settle down. He wanted to run again, and I couldn't blame him.

I was already starting to fight some primal

urges of my own... again. I tried to ignore the feeling of my loincloth shrinking around me, but I found myself shifting uncomfortably as my barely restrained erection rubbed into the small of my sheleki's back.

Keep it together. I cannot afford to lose focus now.

The rain intensified as we crept along the ridge through the thin trees, and I heard another crash off in the distance.

Voices started to crackle over the comm unit again, and I turned it down to keep anyone but me from overhearing it.

The cyborg muttered, "There's little in this direction besides Gladiator territory, unless they're going past it to Tarsis."

I was getting too used to that soulless growl of a voice, and I ground my teeth as I kept listening in.

"But, sir, we still can't breach Gladiator lands without permission." Whoever the male was, he sounded nervous and exhausted.

"Since when have we ever let those filthy animals' laws stop us? I don't care if those beastly creatures outnumber us. We have better technology and a right to retrieve our stolen property."

I stifled a growl. *Property? My mate is not yours. I'll kill you and all your warriors for hunting her—us—like prey.*

I stared coldly out at the gaps between the trees as we made our way across the end of the ridge, barely able to make out the faint glow of the hovercraft lights far below us. Their chatter grew more sporadic; maybe they decided to hunker down in the rain. The group that had been following us had to break off for just that reason.

Finally, hard, stinging hail began to fall, and Brax ran the last hundred yards, galloping all out toward that thick patch of trees. Over the communicator, I could hear cursing and Belland's shouted orders.

That's what you get for relying on hover vehicles in a region known for its storms. Fools. There's a reason we use dogs.

But their leader didn't seem to care about the danger he was sending his men into or ordering the reinforcements to get into position in the valley below us. This cyborg was not a man with honor. And when I killed him—and I would kill him— I would rip him apart, leaving his body for the wild animals so he would have more good use in death than he'd had in life.

We finally reached the dense patch of forest, and I steered us inside and brought Brax to a stop. I had chosen a small bower within a ring of *shan* trees, their dull red fruit hanging within reach. Some were still whole, and I made a note of them for later when we were calmer.

The canopy was so thick that the water barely dripped on us. Now and again, though, a big enough hailstone made it through and slammed into the ground or bounced off one of the nearby trunks. I could feel Ella trembling in my arms, and I brushed my fingers through her hair comfortingly. My Wulfaen was irate and distressed by the scent of fear that clung to our female... and so was I. My beast clawed me from the inside, fighting to get out—to shift—to go after the cyborg and his team. And destroy the source of our mate's anguish.

Swallowing over the lump of rage that threatened to consume me from the inside out, I growled, "We hide here."

I hated hiding. I disliked that we had been forced to do it so often in our escape. But I was outnumbered by the small army after us. Not that my Wulfaen or I could not overpower and kill them. If circumstances had been different, we could and would—if I had been alone.

If the catchers had just been after me, I would have shifted into my Wulfaen, making quick work, killing all of the catchers, and been done with this ridiculous chase long ago. But I had Ella to protect, and shifting into my beast would have left her vulnerable—to one of the catchers sneaking in and snagging her— while I fought and killed the team.

No. I cannot shift. Not when I had to shield Ella from all attempts to steal her from me.

I must remain on the offense, watching, defending, staying a few steps ahead of the cyborg. Keeping Ella alive and out of our enemy's grip.

If that meant huddling in a muddy grove until backup came from my pack, that was what I would do. I refused to whine about it. I had far too much at stake—the life of my precious mate—to waste any energy complaining.

"Ella, we send Brax." I jumped down and offered two hands to help her down. "He bring help." I prayed I was getting my meaning across. She stared at me, then nodded slowly, dismounting with my assistance.

Working together, we removed Brax's pack and gear, including his saddle. He whined and nosed me worriedly as I removed his collar, and I patted him reassuringly.

I couldn't send any kind of automated message. It would be tracked too easily now. But a dog could go undetected where machines could not. I hastily recorded a message on one of the crystals I had left.

"Elders, we are pinned down at the near end of the Valley of Flowers. A company of slavers stands between us and our sector. I request extraction for two. Teken."

I clipped the tube into Brax's ruff and patted him. "Go home, Brax. Go home."

He looked back at me once, then thudded his tail against a tree trunk as he caught on. He bolted forward, running through the semi-dark of the storm, crossing the valley at the wooded end, and then racing on toward sector lands.

Ella tugged on one of my arms gently, and I wrapped all four around her.

"When... help?" she asked in a worried tone with a lot of chatter between the human words I knew.

"Soon." I reassured her and hoped I was right.

CHAPTER 27

ELLA

A THUNDERSTORM STRUCK RIGHT after Brax went bounding off with his message. I wished I knew where exactly he was going and how long we would have to wait for a response. Teken and I had no problem communicating on a deeper level, but we couldn't get a lot of everyday concepts across.

I didn't know what Battle City was, but if Teken had friends there, I wanted to get there as soon as possible. If anyone around here could be trusted, it was him—and I prayed that extended to his friends as well.

I just hoped the big doggy did a good job getting the message to them. Meanwhile, we were stuck in a muddy area with a storm raging and a small army of hunters looking for us.

The thunder boomed and rolled through the valley as the black clouds hammered the ground with hail. The air was warm, the moist breezes blowing pleasantly through the foliage, but the thunder and flashes of lightning made me jump.

I'm tough, but I'm also damn tired of cages, hostile aliens, and running.

Teken wrapped both sets of arms around me and bent over me, taking the few hailstones that made it through the canopy and onto his broad back. Now and again, he grunted slightly and jerked, the only sign of his discomfort.

I wondered once again why Teken had come to rescue me in the first place. He couldn't have been at the compound on a shopping trip for earthlings. He had to have been pretending to be there for something else. *But what?*

I really wished I had the damn translator. But we had bigger problems to deal with as we huddled in the brush. I longed to speak clearly with him right now. Learning a language was slow going, and here we were, falling for each other without one in common. Not to mention, I was a stranger to this whole world—a human who was now a fugitive.

Teken seemed determined to get me somewhere—hopefully outside my captors' range of influence. *But what will happen after that? Do Teken and the Gladiators have the ability to get me back to Earth?*

I missed Mom, home, and the comfortable life I'd made in New York. But I knew that once I was back on Earth, I'd miss Teken like crazy.

Teken is the man I've been searching for all my life.

He made me laugh when all I wanted to do was cry.

He kissed and comforted me at all the right moments.

Teken worked hard to make me happy, protecting me at all times.

And he attempted to understand me, despite the communication issues.

I want—no, need—to spend more time getting to know him, not leave him.

Shit. Now, I'm torn between the life I left behind on Earth and the new one that I'm creating with him. Fuck. I'm falling in love with an... alien. And he seems to be falling in love with me.

But what if I'm wrong about his feelings for me? What if there's no chance in hell of our staying together because the slavers will chase me if I remain?

It infuriated me that the Omers still had more women captive back at their facility that they were priming to sell. There was no way in hell I could just tuck tail and run back to Earth without saving every female the Omers had in their clutches.

I didn't know how, but I was going to rescue all of the hostesses and shut down the Omers. *Would Teken and his people be willing to help me?*

I bit my bottom lip. I didn't know anything about the Gladiators as a race. *I only know Teken, and he's a good man. But is he an anomaly among the Gladiators?*

Just because Teken had integrity and a good heart didn't mean his people did. Maybe he didn't condone the atrocities of slavery, and his people did. This new notion seemed to fit why Teken rescued me and was now protecting me from the slavers. But this was all conjecture. I didn't have all the facts about the

Wulfaen Gladiators or Teken. And I didn't have a chance in hell of figuring out any of this crap until we could communicate properly.

I hoped that things turned out okay between us when we finally had a real conversation. But I feared the worst. That my alien lover belonged to his world and I to mine. That there was no future for us together.

I didn't want to dwell on the elephant in the room—that once I got a translator, the cocoon that surrounded our budding romantic relationship would burst and we'd realize all we had was phenomenal sexual chemistry and nothing else.

But I didn't want to think about that looming heartbreak. I wanted to stay in the honeymoon phase. Maybe after we got safely to his home, we could go somewhere together for a couple weeks. Someplace beautiful, like the scenes from the screens back at that terrible place. Teken could fuck my brains out, and we could relax for a while before dealing with the world and reality.

Could we do that? Probably not.

"Teken," I said quietly.

He unfolded himself from around me,

holding up a broad palm first to make sure the hail had stopped falling, and then moved around in front of me.

"Yes?" he replied huskily.

"We go to Battle City," I said slowly in English. He nodded. Then I spread my hands. "What then?"

He touched his ear and then mine, indicating where the translator device had been removed. "You... me. Talk."

"We talk," I repeated. He nodded, and my heart sank a little. He didn't look entirely comfortable with the idea either.

I spoke up again. "What then?"

He frowned, then switched to his own language. I could only understand a few words. "You... Free... Choice."

"You say... I choose what's next. Me." I laid a hand against my sternum, and he nodded enthusiastically, spreading a hand toward me.

"You my mate. You my world," he said with sudden, strange clarity and then repeated it in his own language, from what I could tell. "But you choose."

I looked up at him, then cupped his face and kissed him. I didn't have the words to tell him that I wanted to sort out a way for us to stay together. I just didn't know if it was possible or if he felt the same. But he stared at me tenderly when our kiss broke, so maybe he did.

"We'll figure this out." I reassured him, not certain if he fully understood me.

He opened his mouth to answer when the earpiece he had taken squawked suddenly. He clapped a hand to his ear, and his eyes widened.

"Ella!" he snapped quietly.

I stiffened and reached for the energy pistol stuck through my belt. *Not now, dammit!*

But too late. Now that the storm was clearing, I heard the whine of the hoverbikes cycling up. One or two sounded like they were getting nearer.

He wrapped his arms around me and pulled me deeper into the bower, away from the stacked belongings, gently laying two fingers across my lips. I nodded, letting him draw me back into the shadows.

Moments later, a dark shape flashed past the tree line, and a familiar throbbing light passed over us. *The scanners. Shit.* I froze—and heard a faint beep.

The dark shape came to a stop and hovered there, its fans rustling the foliage near it.

Come on. Don't notice us. Just move on.

The scanner beam flashed over us again, and my stomach plummeted with fear.

No, no, don't. Just leave us alone.

Teken pointed his stolen energy rifle at the shadow, while I pointed my pistol. Both of us were stiff with tension. His lower arms stayed around me. When the beam touched me, he tensed as if he wanted to block it from my skin like the hailstones.

Long heartbeats passed... and then the scanner swept over us a third time, and I heard that same faint beep.

Oh fuck.

I felt Teken's muscles tighten, and then the figure on the hoverbike started to shout something.

We both fired at once. The shots hit the bike broadside. Its rider toppled off with a scream, and it burst into flames and dropped out of sight, trailing sparks and smoke. I heard the terrible hum of electricity arcing and then a heavy *whoomph* as the whole thing went up.

Teken shouted something and then dragged me backward into the forest. I got my feet under me and ran with him as he bounded into the depths. He helped me along, sometimes carrying me over tree roots or fallen logs too high for me to jump.

When my lungs started burning and my legs ached, I heard the noise of the hoverbikes growing louder and louder. I forced myself to keep moving. The catchers were converging on us. They couldn't go fast or enter the canopy in most spots. That meant their scanners wouldn't work once they lost sight of us. But I could hear them overhead, getting closer.

I could see another bower ahead, this one with much older trees and draped heavily with vines. I put on a burst of speed, but suddenly, inexplicably, Teken shouted something in his own language and stopped dead.

The hover engines seemed to be all around us, coming closer and closer.

"Teken!" I hissed at him, wondering what he saw ahead that had made him stop.

Suddenly, Teken scooped me up again and threw himself to the side, rolling with me beneath the arch of a gigantic tree root. I froze, and a dark shape flashed down from a gap in the trees, its engines whining. It went right past where we had been running and onward into the vine-draped area beyond.

My eyes widened as I realized why Teken had stopped so abruptly. I stared ahead and saw the man dragged off his hoverbike by dozens of leafy tentacles. The man let out a shriek, and the hoverbike shot on by itself, slamming into a tree and bounding off it to dig a trench in the dirt just beyond.

"A deathtrap." I gasped. And we'd almost run right into it.

Behind us, we heard the sudden sound of energy rifle fire and then the heavy thud of an explosion. I looked back and saw a chunk of jungle disappear into burning shreds. Then two hoverbikes dropped into the gap.

Teken turned back to the tentacle-filled grotto and fired two shots into its midst. The tentacles all retracted, a few twitching and burning while their owners shrieked thinly. Then he did another crazy thing; he ran straight into their center.

Before I knew it, I was being carried fireman-style through a path full of monsters, while the remaining tentacles darted after us eagerly. Bikes raced toward us as if they couldn't see the danger. I started firing my pistol at the groping green tendrils.

My eyes squinted painfully against the glare as I shot at everything that moved, the pistol starting to warm up uncomfortably after the seventh shot. I kept going as Teken ran, sometimes firing his rifle ahead of us to try to clear a path.

We ran past the man being ripped apart by vines and his burning hoverbike. I heard the screams of the two hoverbike pilots plowing into the mess behind us and being grabbed as well. I caught the heavy thuds of their bikes crashing. We ran toward the far edge of the deadly grotto, both of us grunting in pain from every shot as our weapons heated in our hands.

Terrified, I clung to Teken as he got us out of the grotto and into the thin sunlight beyond. He put me down, and we ran together, headed across a stand of saplings to the far ridge on the other side. I kept the pistol handy, grateful at least that I had a chance to let it cool before I fired it again.

We were halfway through the saplings when an energy bolt was fired practically at my feet. Teken skidded to a stop with me, and we fired in that direction. A hoverbike's engine faltered, and I heard someone curse and then a heavy thud.

We kept running. My lungs could barely catch sips of air now. My thighs felt weighted by lead, and my body throbbed and ached with the effort of moving. But as the banshee hum of the hoverbikes descended toward us through the trees, I knew we had run out of hiding places.

Teken stopped again, drawing his other pistol. He exchanged a hard glance with me, and I nodded. There was no more running. Now we fought, or we would not survive.

Perhaps taught a lesson by their companions' fates, the rest of the cyborg's team used rappelling gear to drop from the canopy. Unfortunately for them, that made them pretty good targets as they descended toward the ground.

I noticed that the energy beams they were firing at us had changed color. They were now an electric purple and dimmer. They didn't seem to damage anything or even kick up dirt as they hit the ground. But I didn't know what their beams would do to Teken or me.

I shot to kill at the dozen or so men diving toward us, and they fired that purplish energy back—warning shots. The catchers seemed to have changed strategy, and they wanted us alive. But we didn't care. We continued to shoot to kill, and that we did when four went down lifeless and others were wounded. There was a loud sound. Then I saw a huge familiar figure join them—the cyborg.

He stared down at me through the red lenses of that otherwise featureless mask, aiming his rifle carefully. Not waiting for him to get off a shot, I fired wildly at him, my gun burning my hand so badly that I dropped it. Fortunately, Teken saw him, too, and opened on him, hitting the cyborg in two of his arms as the mechanical-faced mercenary bounded off the trees to dodge shots. As the cyborg swung past, he aimed at me again, and my whole world went purple.

My eyelids slid closed as a bolt of energy raced through me.

Fuck. This is it. I'm dying.

But strangely, instead of the cyborg's shot killing or hurting me, my muscles went slack. I couldn't move. My eyes wouldn't open, and my limbs were rag-doll limp. This was some sort of paralysis device.

I fought down my panic. *Breathe, Ella.* I needed to have all my wits about me to survive this shit. But it was disorienting and frightening not being able to see what was going on around me.

Teken shouted. Then there were the sounds of weapons being fired. The mercenary yelled something in his harsh voice, and suddenly, all firing ceased.

What the hell is going on?

Fear twisted my stomach when I felt myself being carried. My eyelids twitched. Then I was able to open them. I sighed with relief that it was Teken lugging me over to a tree. Once we arrived, he set me down with my back against the rough surface. Lifting my hand, he took my pulse and, seeming satisfied with what he felt, his other hand smoothed back my hair. He nodded with a grim face before letting go and getting to his feet. He shouted something to the slave catchers in an abrasive tone.

It sounded like a challenge.

Yes! Give 'em hell, Teken.

CHAPTER 28

TEKEN

WHEN THE STUNNER beam hit Ella and she went limp, I felt it right in my chest through our faint mate connection.

I was terrified that the cyborg had miscalculated and killed her.

Then I saw her breathing steadily, and I relaxed a little.

For hours as we fled, I had defied my physical instincts and focused on our forming mate connection. It was like an invisible string that tethered us together; it wasn't strong, but it was there. Now we were caught, and another instinct had risen within me to shift into my beast. But I'd exerted too much energy already, and the time it took to shift would leave her unprotected and at the mercy of the catchers.

The cyborg was smart and waited for me to get distracted, to make a mistake. He wanted to steal Ella and make a mad dash back to the Omers. But I was smarter than all of them. I was an alpha. A Wulfaen. And the cyborg was not taking my mate from me.

"Anyone who comes near her will die," I threatened in a cold, firm voice. "You will never take her back with you."

Belland snorted as he touched down. His wounded arms were crawling with medical nanites. I wondered if they were embedded in his cyber systems or if he just kept vials of them handy.

He kept his stunner aimed at me even as he held up his other set of arms placatingly. "Let's be reasonable..." His eyes narrowed. "Gladiator," he spat.

I stiffened. He figured out my race. Now I would have to kill every male here, along with any reinforcements that showed up. Every-one. It could not get back to the slavers that the Gladiators were involved in any capacity;

this would cause war between the Omers and us. My actions were mine alone, and I could not drag the entire Gladiator race into a war that was not of their choosing. I had to clean up this mess with the Omers and catchers on my own... and hopefully with the assistance of my pack—if Brax got to them at all with my message.

"Yes." Belland continued. "I know you're a Wulfaen. You gave it away by heading toward the one sector that is inhospitable to anyone but your own kind. You could have headed to the outposts, but you did not. Besides, your evasion skills are too good for a common bandit." He paused with a smirk. "Look. I want no trouble with you, Wulfaen. Just walk away. Leave us the earthling, and we'll forget this incident ever happened."

"No," I barked.

The cyborg frowned. "You've stolen the property of my employers without paying and without her being safely conditioned. Humans are unpredictable and dangerous. She could easily turn on you."

I barked, "My female will not, and she does not need conditioning." I eyed him cautiously. "She is my mate. She belongs with me, and you will not harm her." I kept glancing back and around to make sure none of his handful of remaining men tried to flank me or slip close to where Ella lay helpless.

"She is not yours," the cyborg snapped.

I stared at him silently. I had no intention of arguing about what I knew was fact—Ella was my one true mate.

"And I have no intentions of harming her," Belland replied. His flat-faced mask with its staring eyes only made his tone all the more creepy and dissonant. "That's bad for business, after all. The damaged ones sell for less. But I'm afraid I'll have to differ with you on one point. She belongs to the Omers."

One of the catchers rushed me, and I shot him in the chest. He gagged and fell over. I ignored the heat of my rifle's power pack blistering my hands and swept my aim around at the rest of them. Two more stopped short and backed off.

"You can't kill us all," Belland chuckled. "But you can walk out of this alive—if you hand over the female. My boss would not want trouble with your pack. From what I've heard, the Omers want to do business with the Gladiators. You buy their earthling females, and all will be forgiven. Now... hand her over."

"I will not," I growled. "She is my mate—"

Belland scoffed. "She is not your mate. This female is wanted by the Omers. She is defective. They have more that you can choose from, but this one is coming back..." He eyed her pointedly. "With me."

"No," I snarled, raising my rifle.

Everyone aimed at me at once. The cyborg was clever. Now that he knew I was a Gladiator, he would not kill me for fear of angering the Omers. It was a known fact that spilling a Gladiator's blood—especially on our land—was a declaration of war with my people. The Omers were also greedy, and war was bad for their business.

"Gladiator, have your actions been sanctioned by your alpha?" Belland asked.

"That is not your business," I spat.

"So that's a no." Belland smiled. "You look like a lower-ranked warrior, so I assume you have not heard about the deal the Omers have made with the alphas of all packs."

I knew that was a lie. The council had voted not to buy from the Omers. And I was the deciding vote that made it so.

The cyborg continued. "You're messing up their deal with your rebellious actions."

"You know nothing," I barked.

"I know that your people will die without the females the Omers own. Do you want that on your head?"

I remained silent, plotting how many of them I could take out without giving them an opening to snatch Ella.

Belland snapped, "She's a whore."

I kept glaring at him. "Watch your accursed mouth, or I'll rip your tongue out."

The whole time, I prayed to every god I could name that Brax had reached the elders with my message and that our reinforcements were on their way. I had cut down a good number of the slave catchers, but Belland and a few others were still standing and he could call for his own reinforcements.

Belland put his lower hands on his hips. "Well, you're certainly being dramatic enough about it. But I suppose your first taste of a female did that to you. Part of why I never touch the slaves myself." He gestured toward my limp Ella casually. "You'll get over her."

"I'll tear the limbs from the first man who touches her." I holstered the pistol and drew my swords even as I kept the rifle aimed. "You will not be able to shoot me down before that man dies."

"And then you will be dead, and what will be the point?" Belland sneered.

"Well…" I started. "Then try to kill me."

"You know I can't risk that, Gladiator," the cyborg replied. "I've only been authorized to bring the earthling back, not start a bloody war with your people." He paused. "But you know that already. One drop of your blood spilled and my bosses will have my head."

Just like I thought… Killing me was not an option.

"Just give up the human," Belland pleaded. "If you wanted her so bad, you could have offered to pay and left through the front door."

"I do not buy females, and neither will my people."

The cyborg scoffed. "You have been misinformed, Gladiator. Sectors one and two have already ordered many females. The Omers's transaction with your alphas is a done deal."

A done deal? I stiffened. *How dare the alphas go against the council's wishes?*

I stared back at him defiantly. "This female is mine, and I am hers," I said. "You will not take her back to that torture complex."

"I'm not going anywhere," Belland shouted. "Not without her."

I positioned my body in a manner that gave me plenty of space both to fight and to protect Ella from anyone who attempted to bypass me to get to her. I pointed one of my swords at him in challenge. "Then come and fight me one on one so at least some of your men will survive this day."

"Well, I can see you're not going to be reasonable. Too bad. I know you Gladiators have admirable combat skills. But they won't win the day for you now." He gestured idly, and two of his catchers rushed me at once.

I tossed the rifle into the air and lashed out with my blades, thwarting a knife thrust and a flurry of blows with my upper arms. I was quick with my blades, slashing open their bellies with two strokes, then spinning as they stumbled. With the strength of the beast within me, I easily cut off their heads. The plasma-tempered steel sang with the impact, both blades shedding drops of gore as they finished their arcs, their surfaces too fine and slick to stay dirtied.

My upper hands caught my rifle and aimed it back at Belland. As I went back to the guard position, I saw him standing very still.

"That's some pretty nice fighting, Gladiator," he growled. "It seems I've underestimated your dedication to keeping this female."

One of his men took a step forward, and Belland immediately raised a hand. "No. Leave this to me. He's too dangerous."

You have no idea.

Inside, I was aflame. The mating urge had burned up in a fire of this cyborg's making. I felt the killing fury race through me uncontrollably. My beast pushed against my skin, fighting to get out. I shoved him down deep inside. The Wulfaen was hard to kill, but a shot to the head by the cyborg's weapon would be fatal.

I was a skilled warrior—the strongest and best in my pack. I could kill them all with ease. I could see the fear in his eyes. He did not want to fight me. But I was the only obstacle in his way, preventing him from snatching Ella.

"We'll see how useful you'll be to your pack once I hew off a few of your arms," Belland replied with a sneer and stowed his stunner. I watched him move toward me slowly, blades emerging from the bracers on his wrists. "I may not have your showmanship, but I'll still cut you into pieces!"

Highly unlikely. "You are welcome to try, you faceless beast."

I set aside the rifle and moved forward eagerly, aware of the threat of his shorter blades but refusing to let that stop me. His weapons did not have the reach or the quality of mine. The right-hand blow from one of my swords would snap, or at least badly damage, one of his. Once I had him partially disarmed, I could go on full offense.

The cyborg lunged forward, and steel rang against steel. He grunted in surprise as I dodged and parried my way around his attacks. And then I kicked him hard in the stomach. Belland staggered back. I slashed at his head, and he barely managed to block clumsily.

"You don't even train daily anymore, do

you?" I chided him as I pressed the attack. "All those metal implants don't make up for lack of skill." I turned aside from another set of his attacks and then used leverage to steer him into a tree.

He caught himself and turned back on me, fumbling for the pistols on his belt. I lunged for him, forcing him to counter hastily —and drop one of his weapons. I pressed in again and propelled him away from it, then kicked it off into the bushes behind me.

"Are you that insecure in your melee skills, slave catcher? Are you perhaps unaccustomed to quarry that does not cower and cry at your approach?"

My eyes darted to Ella, ensuring she was safe. Surprisingly, her eyes were open, and she was stirring slightly. Maybe I had absorbed some of the energy of the blast for her by trying to shield her with my body. But whatever it was, she looked back at me, and her hand crept toward the pistol in the dirt beside her.

"Shut up!" Belland snapped, slashing at me again.

I deflected three of his blows, grabbing his arm as he went for the lunge, twisting his limb brutally with my upper arms. He hissed with pain as the bone broke. One arm and weapon down.

I threw him backward against a tree. "Enough of this. Submit and die an honorable death," I ordered.

"No deal."

I heard hoverbikes overhead as another handful of exhausted-looking men started dropping from the canopy on lines. When they landed, they stood with the others and watched. They probably feared the repercussions of interfering in their leader's fight against me.

I knocked Belland away into a tree again and checked on Ella while he recovered. She winked at me, her eyes gleaming with pride.

Heartened, I turned back to my opponent, who had recovered more quickly than expected and was already lunging toward me again. I grunted in pain as his blades slammed into the flat of mine. He tried to tangle my legs up at the same time, and we lurched across the tiny clearing together, struggling and cursing.

I felt one of his blades score my ribs, and I growled, shoving him off me and then slashing him across his chest armor. The shoulder belt across his armor's front snapped apart, fell, and sparks flew from the chest plate beneath. Belland grunted.

"Boss?" asked one of the others, stepping forward.

"Stay back. I've got this animal," Belland growled warningly.

His subordinate nodded and stepped back.

I heard a rustle near Ella, and I trusted that she had her sidearm back. *Good. If I fall, she at least has a chance of defending herself.*

"Answer me this," I demanded in a clear tone as Belland panted for air. He was a bully, not a warrior, and therefore not fit for prolonged fights.

"Even if you beat me, my warriors will cut you down and take her anyway," the cyborg gloated. "And they'll patch me up good as new."

"Will they give you a whole new head, then?" I retorted, lashing out with my blades and forcing him to duck and stumble back. "I'll put my blade through your brain to make sure they can't just stick it in some other abomination."

I lunged again, whirling my blades, targeting his other arm. He didn't quite get out of the way fast enough. Blood sprayed as his flesh splayed open.

He yelled with pain and fury.

Stepping in, I swung my sword with all my might. It struck metal and bone. Its song became a harsh screech as it turned slightly on the rim of his steel collar and then slammed into his mask beneath his cheekbone.

He staggered back, holding his face, and I saw part of the mask drop off under his hand, revealing a bloody scowl. "You stupid, disgusting Gladiator." He snarled. "Do you really want to die for some human whore?"

"You seem to forget who is losing this fight," I snapped as I drove my knee up through his shattered armor and into his gut. He doubled over. I spun past him and brought one blade down two-handed on his spine—killing him.

There was a collective gasp from his team. One catcher raised his rifle, and Ella sat forward, shooting him through the heart.

I straightened, ribs hurting, arms covered

in small cuts and bruises, and unslung my rifle.

I heard running feet crashing through the brush nearby. My heart sank, thinking Belland had more reinforcements. The handful of warriors left must have thought so, too, because they relaxed slightly and leveled their rifles at us again.

Before firing could start, a massive black streak bounded past me and slammed into two of the soldiers. Screams erupted. They were still attached to their wires, so they couldn't run as Brax made short work of them.

Shouts erupted to accompany the running feet. I heard the battle cries of my pack and raised my voice to join them. I sighed with relief when a dozen of my brethren warriors burst over the rise on the backs of their riding dogs.

The battle was bloody but quick. The last of the slave catchers died without getting a single shot off.

I sheathed my weapons and hurriedly turned to Ella, who was slowly pulling herself to her feet along the tree trunk.

"Ella!" I tried to remember the correct words in her language. "You right?" Helping her up, I hugged her tightly, burying my nose into her hair and inhaling deeply. My female was safe.

She squeezed me back as hard as she could, careful to avoid my gashed ribs.

Ferion asked, "What is happening, Alpha?"

I was happy to see my beta and closest childhood friends.

I released Ella from our hug but clutched her protectively by my side so that my pack could see their alpha female. "There is much to tell once we get back to our sector," I replied.

Ferion sniffed the air loudly, and his eyes widened. "You are now mated? To the human female?"

"Yes. She is my sheleki," I said gravely, watching my pack exchange astonished looks. "The gods have honored me with my one true mate."

My men bowed to Ella.

My mate waved at them but remained silent.

I started. "Her name is Ella. She has full memory of her time among the slavers. She could act as a witness against the Omers and their dirty actions."

"That is good news, Alpha," Ferion answered with a grim expression. "Because the elders have received distressing news about sectors one and two. Both alphas have gone against the council's decision and purchased earthlings from the Omers. We've been informed that the females are currently en route to their packs."

This was not good news. "And sectors four and five?" I asked.

"They have declared war on one and two."

"I will deal with this problem when I get my mate back to our pack. She needs food, rest, and a translator unit. Hers is no longer working properly."

I looked down at Ella, who seemed mostly recovered. I kissed the top of her head, and she smiled up at me before going back to considering my warriors and their pack of now quite curious riding dogs.

Brax padded over with his tail wagging and snuffled us both carefully, licking my wound—that was already healing—before crouching in front of us. He had fresh gear. I would have to go back for the cache I had left, but right now, I was too exhausted to care.

I gently helped Ella onto Brax's back. Ferion looked between us and frowned.

"Are you telling me that you spent this entire time unable to speak, but you still managed to establish your mating? How?" He sounded completely baffled.

I slapped him on the back. "There are plenty of ways to communicate with a female that do not require words."

His eyebrows shot toward his hairline, and a ripple of laughter ran through my brethren. "I need a mate," Ferion replied, causing more laughter.

"Patience, my brothers. As it turns out, nothing too exotic is needed to appeal to human females. Just good treatment, honor, and the use of all one's hands in bed."

They were still chuckling as we turned for home, the dogs bounding eagerly along the path beyond the valley. I held Ella as we rode. She sagged against me, bone tired.

I rode in deep thought. *Will what I have to offer Ella really be enough to keep my mate with me?* I felt a cold lump in my stomach at the notion that she might decide to walk away from me... from us.

The fight to defeat Belland was nothing compared to the trial ahead to win Ella's heart. And I could not—no, would not—fail in demonstrating with both actions and words how much she meant to me and the joy and happiness she brought into my life.

CHAPTER 29

ELLA

"DOES THAT FEEL ALL RIGHT?" The Gladiator medic sat back after fastening the translator in place in my ear.

I looked back at him and nodded. "Yes."

"All right." He smiled. "Can you understand me?"

"I can," I replied.

He extended a small, jewel-tipped probe to touch the translator. "Again?" he demanded.

"Yes, I understand you," I answered.

"Excellent." He nodded. "Now it is properly calibrated." He stood and helped me up. "The good news is you have no lasting bodily damage from your ordeal with the Omers.

Given time, the psychological effects should fade quickly, especially if you avoid stressful situations such as extreme confinement. The slavers already inoculated you against local diseases. But if you feel any illness, don't hesitate to come to me, all right?"

"Thank you, doctor." I smiled.

"It's my honor, Alpha Sheleki." He bowed.

The title made me uncomfortable, given that Teken and I had only been here for twelve hours and still hadn't ironed out anything between us. Most of that time we'd spent sleeping or making love in his chambers. Finally, the translator I needed arrived, and here I was getting my fitting.

"Doctor, just call me Ella. I'm not big on titles."

"And you can call me Kylene. Doctor is way too formal." He grinned. "And please tell the alpha that he's due for a visit. Even though the shift normally takes care of the healing process, I still need to verify that all is well."

Kylene escorted me out of his small clinic located in one of the many dwellings in the large, open space they called the central courtyard. I stood, quietly observing Teken perched on top of the ledge that overlooked a huge pen that held riding dogs like Brax that were being trained by Gladiators.

Teken was tall, brawny, and rough around the edges but simply magnificent as he laughed at something one of his men said.

It really wasn't a surprise that he was a leader—the alpha—given his confidence, badass fighting skills, intelligence, and strategic craftiness in keeping us alive. What caught me off guard was the sheer number of Gladiators that he ruled, fifty of them in total. And from what I'd seen so far, his warriors respected him and looked to him for guidance and wisdom.

After our battle with the slavers and their ultimate death, Teken was very silent on the trek back to his home. So was I. Both of us were lost in thought after our nail-biting ordeal was over.

And once we'd arrived at his sector, I'd become overwhelmed by the throng of Gladiators that rushed to welcome him back home. And when they laid eyes on me, I could have heard a pin drop. It was obvious they'd never seen a human before.

During the awkward silence, Teken had

pinned me against his side protectively and said, "Sheleki." The one word transformed their expressions, which ranged from shock to confusion to wonder. But thankfully, I'd seen no hostility and sensed no malice from anyone in the crowd, which, frankly, was a big relief.

My thoughts snapped back to the present when I spotted Teken striding toward me.

"Ella!" he cried softly as he laid two big, gentle hands on my shoulders. "Is it done? Can you understand me?"

My chest tightened, and I was nervous about our first "real" conversation. Now it was time to get to know each other on a deeper level.

After an awkwardly silent moment of collecting myself, I answered, "Yes, Teken. I can understand you perfectly."

His expression went from hopeful to just a touch nervous, his smile fading. "Excellent. Then we should go back to my chambers to talk in private. Yes?"

It was bizarre to hear him speak in complete sentences after days of single words, noises, and gestures. I was getting to know his mind as well. He sounded like a Roman-era scholar-warrior, his speech even a little formal.

"Yes. That would be nice," I said breathlessly, taking one of his hands, giving it a gentle squeeze.

He smiled at me tenderly before whisking me across the courtyard.

The Gladiators that passed us bowed their heads to Teken and said, "Alpha." And to me, they said, "Alpha Sheleki."

"Wulfaen," Teken replied before giving them a wide smile.

"Hello," I greeted.

So far, with every Gladiator I'd met, their vibe had been welcoming, though it was strange and sad not to see any females around. And every so often, I'd catch the wistfulness in some of their eyes. It seemed to be a longing for the companionship that Teken had found with me. But there was never a moment that I sensed any jealousy. In fact, they made me feel relaxed and safe.

We strolled by the market stalls full of strange and colorful fruit, vegetables, and other things that seemed odd in shape. Finally out of the courtyard, we strode down the dirt path that sliced through several rows of large, stone-façade homes.

We remained silent. There was a tension between us, as if we were each carrying a huge load of saved-up words that we feared might spill out publicly if we let even a few slip out. Yet we still held hands and related gently to one another, as if this new thing between us wasn't in peril at all.

Once outside his massive stone home, I widened my eyes at the items bound in decorative cloth and piled at the entrance. All of the objects were so carefully wrapped that they looked like gifts.

"What's all this?" I turned to eye him. "Is it your birthday?" *Oh, please say no... I'll feel like shit because I don't have a birthday gift for you.*

Teken sighed heavily, releasing my hand and scooping up the items. "Come inside, Ella, and I'll explain."

We both entered his chambers and walked into his kitchen, where he placed the parcels on a hook. He grabbed my hand, ushering me to sit on one of the two ornate wooden chairs that surrounded his kitchen table.

We looked at each other like a couple at the end of their first date. Both of us unsure of what to say or do next.

"Ella, you must be hungry. Let me get you something to eat."

"Thank you, Teken." He was right. I was famished.

My appetite had been through the roof. *Must be all those calories I've been burning up during our marathon rounds of sex.* Frankly, between the insatiable need to have sex with Teken all the time and the insistent craving to eat everything in sight, I didn't know what was going on.

He reached out and grazed the side of my cheek with the back of his hand. "Anything for you," he replied before walking over to the shelf that held all the parcels he'd received.

Getting more comfortable, I wiggled my ass on the comfy cushion seat that made sitting on the ornate wooden chair bearable, and I watched as he grabbed two of his gifts and a couple of cups, bringing the items over to the table and placing them on top before taking a seat directly across from me.

He unwrapped one of the bundles—a large platter loaded with some sort of baked goods—and rumbled, "It's tradition among my people to give gifts of food and drink to a mated pair before and after their Wulfaen mating ceremony."

My mouth watered at the sight of the strange-shaped, flaky-looking pastries. They were brightly colored—like dye-dipped Easter eggs—and some had a sugar-like substance on top. *God, I miss scones, cinnamon rolls, doughnuts, and croissants.*

"What is a mating ceremony?" I asked while he unwrapped the other item on the table, revealing a tall, slender steel cylinder container. He popped off the lid, and steam rose. He poured the brown liquid into two large cups. The brew was aromatic like...

Oh sweet baby Jesus. Is that coffee? Please, let it be...

He pushed a cup into my hand and ordered, "Drink, my Ella, before it gets cold."

I took a sip of the concoction and moaned. The liquid was hot and sweet with a slight bitter note. *It's not coffee, but pretty close.*

"What is this?" I inquired between sips.

"We call it *saptru,* and we drink it in the morning or before going into battle. It gives us an extra burst of energy."

That would explain the caffeine-like buzz racing through my veins. "Oh... it's like what humans call coffee, and we also drink it in the morning." I paused. "And the evening... Shit, for coffee lovers like me, I drink it all day long."

"Shit?" Confusion clouded his gaze. "What does that mean?"

I laughed at the adorably perplexed expression on his face. "Shit is a curse word... like swearing..."

His face lit up. "Ah... like *tagah*. This is a bad word we use when things are going wrong."

"Yes. I heard you say it while we were on the run from the slavers."

"Because things were very bad," he answered.

I reached across the table, grabbing his hand. "But it has gone from bad to good, right?"

"Yes, sheleki. It has." He cupped my face with his other hand, and I leaned into it, enjoying his touch.

"So? The ceremony?" I ventured.

I nearly pouted when his hand fell away from my face.

"The mating ceremony is a celebration where the mate pair pledges their life, power, strength, and loyalty to each other." The intensity of his gaze made my clit pulse. "Both swear to cherish and honor each other. And the male promises to protect his female with his life. The vows are read by the pack's elders, and the ceremony takes place before the pack, letting it be known to all Wulfaen that the mated pair vows to stand together until our final breath."

Wait... Is he asking me to marry him?

My eyes widened. "This sounds like what we call a wedding on Earth."

"What is a wedding?" he inquired.

I struggled a little with the words to put it simply. "A couple decides they want to spend their lives together. Then they take months, sometimes years, to plan the ceremony where they go before their friends and family to witness their commitment to love and live with each other until the day they die."

"Yes. That is similar to our tradition. Except when a Wulfaen finds his mate, his heart and inner beast know instantly. He does not wait. He seeks to claim and mark his female immediately."

"Is that why you bit me?" I asked.

He nodded. "Yes. It lets others know you and I are mated for life and we are one. It also warns them there will be hell to pay if they try to hurt you."

I squeaked, "Mated for life?"

"Yes."

My breath caught in my throat as I blinked hard.

There was a lot wrong with him not asking me if I was down for that type of commitment *before* he bit me.

Yes. There was the whole communication issue that prevented him from explaining the mating thing, and... yes, I love him—now. But marriage? What will we do when I go back to Earth?

I swallowed hard. *But do I really want to leave him?*

I didn't... I truly adored the big-hearted alien.

"Teken," I said solemnly. "You didn't ask if I wanted to be mated to you."

"You do not care for me?" he asked in a low tone.

My pulse accelerated at his question.

I was a straight-up type of chick, so I

wasn't about to pussyfoot around when it came to my feelings or his.

"I care about you a lot." I patted over my heart. "I love you. You mean the world to me."

He smiled and patted his chest. "My heart sings for you, too. The youngling in your belly will be big and strong. My Wulfaen chose well, and I will love, care, serve, and protect you and our pup until the day I die."

Wait! What?

My stomach plummeted. "Hold on a minute. Are you saying that I'm pregnant?" We'd had lots of unprotected sex, but it never even crossed my mind that I could now be pregnant with his child—youngling... pup... whatever he called our unborn baby.

He arched a brow. "What is 'pregnant?'"

I huffed, fighting a panic attack. "That my belly"—I jabbed a finger at my stomach—"is filled with a youngling. Or is it a pup?" *Oh Jesus. Me as a mother?*

"Youngling and pup... It is the same thing," he replied simply.

I narrowed my eyes. "And how do you know I'm having a pup?" We'd only been together for days, not months. How could he even know so fast?

He sniffed the air loudly. "I scented the change when you woke up today." He frowned. "Did you not know?" Teken asked, disbelief clear in his expression and tone.

Utterly mystified, I stared at him. "No!" I hissed. "I did not know. Human females often have signs that we're pregnant—but not so soon—and I didn't have any."

The truth of the matter was that even if I'd missed my period, I wouldn't have suspected anything because my cycle wasn't consistent.

"Not for us Wulfaen," he answered. "Our sense of smell is strong, especially when it comes to females."

I crossed my arms over my chest. "Then why didn't Kylene say anything to me about it?"

He shrugged one massive shoulder. "He probably thought you knew. Our females always knew when they were with young."

"Well, I'm human, not a Wulfaen." Then another thought came to me. "Will I birth one pup? Or multiple pups at once?"

I'd always wanted a big family, but never thought I'd find the right man to settle down with. Now I was pregnant with an alien's baby. There was no way I could return to Earth knocked up by Teken. Once humans found out, I would become a freak and so would my baby. Scientists would take my baby away and experiment on my child and me just for the hell of it.

I'd have to get word to Mom that I was here. Maybe she could come visit me.

Teken answered, "Normally, our females have one pup at a time. Not many. But I come from a royal bloodline and my seed is strong, so I do not know. But I would welcome more than one pup." He smiled like the Cheshire cat.

I blinked. "When I give birth, will our pup come out as a furry wolf?" *Jesus.* This was uncharted territory for me.

"Our youngling will come out as a Gladiator. We don't shift into our Wulfaen form until we have lived a couple of cycles. He or she will still be a youngling and will have to be guided by me into their first shift."

I sat still, digesting my new reality. I was going to be a mother to a Wulfaen Gladiator on an alien planet. *Fuck. My. Life.*

"Do not worry, Ella." He patted my hand. "I've instructed Kylene to research everything he needs to nurture your human body in gestating our pup... or pups. And once our ceremony is complete, we will be properly bonded, which will protect you from diseases and give you a longer lifespan." He intertwined our fingers. "We are one, and I will tell the elders that our ceremony will happen tonight."

"Not so fast, Teken," I snapped. "We have a lot more talking to do before that's going to happen."

He shrugged. "So we talk now and have the ceremony tonight."

I sighed heavily. My alien mate was determined to have his way.

He picked up a baked item from the plate, holding it before my lips. "Open, Ella."

"Are you bribing me with food?" I asked, tugging my hand away from his.

"Yes." He grinned. "Is it working?" He waggled his eyebrows.

"No." I made a grab for the morsel of food. He evaded my gesture.

"Ella," he whispered. "It is my honor to feed my female."

His words made me feel all warm and gushy inside. No man had ever cared about me like this alien did. It was flattering, humbling, and welcoming. And there was no doubt in my mind that I loved him dearly, but sometimes his stubbornness made me want to strangle the shit out of him.

Parting my lips, I took a bite of his offering. "It's delicious," I said. It was sweet and crispy—but a little grainy. After a bit of chewing, it melted on my tongue. "What is this scrumptious treat called?"

"It is zupol. Some of the Gladiators are very skilled at creating different types. It is also baked in a very hot pit."

He fed me another piece. After eating it all, I exclaimed, "Well, I love it. I can eat this all day and never get tired of it. So sign me up for more zupol."

His face saddened. "I am not skilled in making zupol, but I do know how to cook very well, Ella. I can take care of you in that manner. Will that make you happy?"

Oh. My. God. He's sad because he thinks he's lacking because he can't bake for me?

I pushed away from the table, striding over to him. "Teken?" I stroked his hair. "You make me happy. I don't care if you can't bake or cook."

He stood, gathering me into his arms. "And you, sheleki, are more female than I deserve."

I curled my fingers and fisted the fabric of his tunic.

He gently nudged me back, giving me a look so full of longing. "I will strive every day to prove that I am worthy of you."

Damn. Damn. Damn. He said the sweetest and most sincere things.

He didn't give me a warning before his hands spanned my waist and he hoisted me high enough to slant his lips across mine. His tongue slid along the seam of my mouth, and I opened to him. His tongue slid over mine, around, seeking every inch of me. A fist in my hair angled my head back, granting him deeper access. His growl vibrated through me, and I clenched my thighs.

He broke off our kiss and said, "Come. We talk more."

I squeaked when he swept me off my feet, striding into the front room. We settled together on a low couch covered in unfamiliar bluish furs. Roughly two seconds later, Brax trotted in from the other room and jumped up with us, panting happily.

I stared at Teken. "So tell me. How did you become the alpha of your pack?"

"The position was given to me when my father died. Only Wulfaen from a royal bloodline are given such an honor. And you, my sheleki, will now be my pack's alpha female."

"But I'm human." I bit my bottom lip.

"A human who is a brave warrior." He smiled. "You are strong. You wouldn't have survived the trek back to my sector if that were not true."

I touched his arm. "Thank you for the compliment."

"It is only the truth," he replied simply. "You have been through so much ill-treatment at the hands of the Omers. And I pledge that they will pay for everything they've done to you."

"I'm not going to lie. It was hell being at their facility, locked up and treated like an animal."

"Ella." He had worry lines between his brows. "I'm not going to ask you about your experiences at the slavers' compound... yet. We can talk about that when you are ready. For now, tell me what you are comfortable revealing."

I sat back against the dog, sighing and pressing my lips together. "Okay. I don't know where to start," I admitted as I looked into his eyes. "When you showed up and offered me a way out, I had to trust you. Not just because I think you're sexy, but because you were the only alien to treat me like a person."

I choked up a little at the end, and he stroked a hand down my hair.

"I live in a big city on Earth. I was visiting my mom in my hometown for the weekend. She must be terrified right now." I rubbed the side of my face, feeling a sudden, stabbing pain in my temple.

Poor Mom. She might have been waiting for word from me for months. "I need to find a way to reach out to her soon."

"This will be difficult, Ella. My people do not have the technology to communicate with or travel to Earth. The truth of the matter is the Reticulans and Omers are the only ones who have transport to Earth."

My heart plummeted. His words confirmed what I'd suspected.

I'll never see or talk to Mom again.

I swallowed hard before saying, "There is no way that I'd trust either of them—even if they were willing—to help me get in contact with my mother."

Knowing the bastards, they would target my mother for retaliation just because she was my family. No. I couldn't risk that.

"Nor would I trust them to provide any transportation to visit her before I give birth to our youngling. The Reticulans and Omers are slavers, and if they ever got their hands on me again, all they would do is either kill me for escaping or sell me on another planet."

"Exactly." Teken nodded with a grim expression. "Both are a greedy race. They care nothing about anyone but themselves and amassing lots of coins. You've already borne witness to how they treat the females they abduct."

I shivered when I thought about the women kept in cages for hours at a time and only let out to use the bathroom and clean their body.

"So," I replied. "There is no way for me to communicate with my mom." It was a statement, not a question.

"I'm so sorry, Ella, but that is correct. But it won't be long before my people find a way to make that happen. We are working every day to advance our technology." He touched my cheek. "Until then, I will make you happy and comfortable within my pack," he promised, and I felt another surge of warmth toward him.

I put on a brave face, refusing to cry over something that could not be fixed easily. Teken said he was working on a solution to getting in contact with Mom, and I believed him. And if I could lend any of my Earth knowledge toward the resolution, then the Gladiators could sign me up for service. Because I would never give up on at least being able to communicate with her again.

"Teken, I love my mom too much to let her worry about me for the rest of her life. So I'll do anything I can to help you and your people find the technology to make contact with Earth. My mom needs to know I'm alive and safe."

"Your happiness is my happiness, sheleki." He ran a finger across my cheek. "So I pledge to never stop working to make sure that happens."

And just like that, he cemented his place within my heart.

"Thank you." I cleared my throat as emotions for my alien choked me. "So... back to my alien experience. I got picked up by these gray aliens, little big-headed guys—the Reticulans. They messed up placing my translator. Something about the wrong battery—um, crystal."

He nodded slowly, frowning. "Reticulans are normally well-known for their technical expertise and for being greedy."

"Well, that explains their lowest-bidder performance." I smiled tightly, and he squeezed my shoulder gently. "Anyway, after that, I went through hell with the Omers—most specifically, an alien I called the overseer."

I shrugged. "You know the rest. They drugged me and stuck me in front of you like a bauble you were considering buying. And then, well, you surprised the shit out of me by helping me escape—and I don't really understand why." I bit my bottom lip. "From what I heard from the Reticulans and the other women at the facility, your race—the Gladiators—made a deal to buy earthlings for sex and to get us pregnant to solve your fertility problem. Is that true?" I stared at him.

"Yes." He confirmed.

I stiffened at his response.

"And no," he said. "Yes. It is true that my race no longer has females to breed with. All of our females died due to being sexually violated and brutalized by the Omers." Steel laced his tone.

I gasped.

He continued. "Before I was born, the Gladiators were once the Omers's slaves. That is until we fought them and won our freedom. During the time of our enslavement, they treated us like animals. The Omers forced our males to remain in their Wulfaen form to fight for sport and coins. And our females were raped by the Omers, who ripped them apart with their incompatible cocks. Those who survived became sick and died. Now, without females, our race will go extinct." He paused. "So when the Omers approached us with a solution—abducted earthling females that were sexually compatible with our race—my people listened..."

All of the pieces to the puzzle were now fitting together.

"Gladiators are desperate to survive," I whispered.

"Yes. Very. But it is more complicated

than that. All Gladiators wait their whole life to find their one true mate."

"Their sheleki," I interjected.

"Yes. Our sheleki. A female who is our other half and is picked only by our inner beast—the Wulfaen." He cupped my cheek. "Without finding our mate, most Gladiators will eventually go feral, shifting into their beast form forever. We call it mating sickness. And when the sickness takes hold, the only thing an alpha can do is hunt down and kill his Gladiator." He shook his head. "The act is hard on the alpha's soul, but it must be done to protect others from the roving, bloodthirsty beast the Gladiator eventually becomes."

Mating sickness? Going feral? Killing their own? So their need to find mates isn't just about a quick fuck. Without their sheleki, these men are doomed for a fatal ending.

"So if they don't find their mate, they will go crazy?" I queried.

"Yes," he muttered.

"Everyone?" I stared at him with my lips pursed in disbelief.

"For some reason, the sickness hasn't touched most of the elders. It's the younger Gladiators who are going feral. We don't understand why. But we know if we don't find a solution, in a few moons, there will be no Wulfaen Gladiators alive."

"Jesus. This is a really bad situation." I bit my bottom lip. "With no females, you'll be decimated, but still... condoning slavery?"

He shook his head. "I don't condone or approve of slavery. Most of us have rejected the solution of buying slaves from the Omers."

"Most?" I arched a brow. "So some of you believe in trafficking females?" I didn't like this ugly truth about the Gladiators. *Do I have to watch my back around the members of his pack?*

"Not anyone in my pack. But unfortunately, even with the Council of Five voting against the plan to buy earthlings, there are some who believe it is the only solution."

"And who or what is the Council of Five?"

"According to Gladiator law, all matters that concern the welfare of the entire Gladiator race have to be voted on by the Council of Five. One alpha from each sector. I am the alpha of sector three. I voted against buying females. So did sectors four and five."

"And one and two?" I couldn't keep the worry and confusion out of my voice.

"They are in favor of buying earthlings. In fact, we just got word that they went against the wishes of the collective council and purchased earthlings that are in transit to their packs as we speak."

Teken shook his head, the look on his face something close to disgust. "Like I said, slavery is not the Wulfaen way. But there is serious strife within the packs about this subject. Gladiators are physically, mentally, and emotionally hurting without a mate."

Anger burned me. "But that's no excuse to allow your race to buy women like property. We have rights. It was not our choice to be abducted from Earth, or whatever planet we lived on, and brought to this planet to be conditioned and dolled up like sex dolls just for the Omers's profit."

"I agree, sheleki. That is why I came to the facility. I was on a mission to gather evidence against the Omers to bring back to the council. I wanted to show them proof of what the Omers were doing to the females... that it was wrong. And after that, I planned to demand a vote to unite all the sectors and shut down the Omers's facility. I will not rest until all of the females are free, Ella."

"Okay. But what about the females who are heading to sectors one and two?" I asked.

"It's being dealt with."

"Good," I gritted out.

"When I arrived at the facility, the first phase of my mission was just to gather evidence." He caressed my face. "But when I saw you, I knew I'd found my one true mate. And I couldn't leave you behind. So I changed my priorities to freeing you and getting you back here to my pack and safety. I still intend to continue with my original plan. Going to the council and demanding that we unite to free all of the females."

"Good. We are in agreement. I want every one of them, human or not, to be freed. I wouldn't wish what happens in that place on my worst enemy."

"Yes." He looked at me earnestly. "But until you were safely out of danger, I could not function at full capacity to complete my mission."

I looked down at my hands. "Will the slavers keep chasing me?"

"No. Once we gather to shut them down

and free the females, we will forbid any such practice. I will not lie to you, Ella. The Omers are very greedy and conniving. Tensions between the Omers and the Gladiators will be high once we take away the females. Maybe they will declare war. I don't know what will happen, but I'm prepared for the worst. I've already sent word to the council that we need to gather for a meeting about the Omers. This meeting will happen in two days and in the Gladiator Capitol."

"I will come with you. I'd like to act as witness to the Omers's treatment."

He reached over and brushed his hand down my back. "I do not want to put you in danger, Ella. Not in your condition, carrying our pup."

My lips pressed into a thin line, and then I said, "Teken, I can't stay here and do nothing. Not with some of the council members supporting buying earthlings. The council needs to see you and me together. They need to understand that finding their mate among the earthlings is still a possibility, but not by buying and breaking her like an animal." I bit my bottom lip, thinking. "And the Gladiators are only sexually compatible with earthlings?"

"Yes," he confirmed.

"And you have a way to get the alien females back to their planets, but not the earthlings?"

"Yes, Ella. Our transport can travel between nearby planets. That is how we travel on business."

"Then what's going to happen to the earthlings that are freed? Where will they go?"

"They will be under the protection of the council. The elders from each pack will oversee the process, that they are taken care of, and if the females wish to visit each pack to see if there is a match with one of our Gladiators, then they are free to do so. But they won't be forced."

My mind was racing with all the possibilities of this shit between humans and Gladiators going wrong. "But the women will need a home to stay in until everything is worked out. May I suggest that the females stay within your pack? It will make them feel safer to be in my presence. They've been through too much already. I'll work with your people to organize living quarters within your pack. I'll be the humans' advocate. This is the only way this union between human females and your people will work. I need to ensure that they are safe and protected."

He smiled. "That is very smart, sheleki. Yes. I will have the elders meet with you to organize everything. And anything you need will be at your disposal." He clasped my hands. "Now, have you decided about our mating ceremony?"

I thought of everything he had been for me before this conversation—rescuer, protector, lover, and now avenger for me and my fellow kidnapped women. I would have to be crazy to turn my back on a man who would do all of that for me. I didn't know how we would work out this weird human-alien romance, but I was as committed as he was to finding a way to make us work.

He chose me. And I chose him. And that was all that mattered.

A smile spread across my face. "I'm ready for our mating ceremony, Teken."

His face lit up, and I suddenly realized with a flush of warmth that he had been fearing I'd reject him.

"Sheleki, you are truly a blessing from the gods." He watched me closely, the look in his eyes making me feel precious and beautiful. "And whatever it takes, Ella, I'll do it to make you happy."

"You already do, Teken. You make me gloriously happy." And I meant it.

He pinned me with his gaze. He stared at me as though he had so much to say and no words to do his thoughts justice. Suddenly, he was holding my face in his hands, and he kissed the ever-loving shit out of me.

I met his kiss with a force of my own. Our tongues swiping, tasting, asking, begging. I pulled away and bit his bottom lip, tugging slightly before I relinquished it. When the kiss was over, we were both out of breath.

"Mate," he said huskily.

His gravelly voice sent vibrations of lust throughout my body.

"Always," I replied, holding his stare.

Being abducted to his world had been a science fiction nightmare, but finding him was the best thing that had ever happened to me.

Teken had my heart, and finding something so genuine in the most difficult and dangerous of situations—as we did—was a rare and beautiful gift.

There was nothing I wouldn't do to be

with my Gladiator... and he to be with his mate and sheleki.

I'd found a partner, lover, friend, and protector in one gorgeous package.

He was truly the love of my life, and I was damn proud to call him my Wulfaen mate.

———

IF YOU LOVED **BEAUTY AND THE ALIEN BEAST**, you're going to devour GALAXY ALIEN WARRIORS, four full-length standalone sci-fi alien romance novels, starring four stubborn human females and four hot Alien Warriors strong enough to master them. Grab GALAXY ALIEN WARRIORS right now.

Disclaimer: the author is not responsible for any actual alien abductions that may result should you purchase this book. ;)

Sign up for my Newsletter to get all my romance releases, sales, sneak peeks and a **FREE** Romance.

SNEAK PEEK AT GALAXY ALIEN WARRIORS

MISTY CHAPTER 1

A faint chime caught my attention as I laced up my favorite purple sneakers. I looked at the small, antique clock hanging in the living room of my sparse Manhattan apartment and smiled. Ten on the nose...the perfect time to go for a run. The air had turned crisp outside, a light breeze freshening it, and the crowds had thinned enough to let me jog without stopping constantly.

Get a move on, Misty.

I was already tired, and if I went out too late, the October night would be too cold to exercise comfortably.

My nightly run was the first part of my three-step plan to unwind after another crazy day of overtime and eating at my desk. Part two would be a long, hot shower. It was Thursday night, so it was time to deep-condition my relaxed, waist-length black hair again. Part three would be pure entertainment. A campy science fiction movie from my collection, a slice of dark chocolate cake, and half a bottle of Chianti would see me through to my bedtime. Perfect, aside from the lack of a fellow night owl to share it with.

New York career women like me often didn't have time to date. We either met someone at work or at one of the places we grabbed food, went looking online, or endured long stretches without company. Usually a combination. I had crappy luck in attracting good men, so I spent a lot of time without a lover.

My last date had been with a Wall Street finance douche who had taken me to an exclusive French restaurant. He had then berated our waitress to the point of tears barely ten minutes after I had met him.

I had watched him enjoy his petty bullying over how the wine had been served for just long enough to see him smile faintly when the server had started sobbing. Then I had excused myself and gone home. Inexpensive wine, meat loaf, and cat videos provided a much better night than Finance Douche would have.

He had blown up my texts with whining and trying to browbeat me into a second date. I had blocked his number, moved on...and reminded myself not even to look at another Wall Street suit again.

I pulled on my oversized purple hoodie and drew up the hood, hiding my hair under it and obscuring some of my curves. It was one of the comfiest things in my wardrobe and—deliberately—one of the least flattering except for the stretchy leggings I wore to run.

I liked my body. Lots of hard exercise in the last few years had turned me from chubby to voluptuous, with strong legs, arms I could go sleeveless with, and an ass I didn't mind looking at in a mirror. The problem was that Manhattan's creepy-guy population all seemed to "like" my body too.

There were a lot of creeps in Manhattan. Young, old, suited, homeless, weasel teenagers in sweatshirts and sideways caps, stumbling drunks, and "upstanding" men wearing wedding rings. They all had one thing in common besides all being male. Way too many of them caught a glimpse of a thick ass and double-D boobs and immediately decided to make pests of themselves...or worse.

I wore headphones on the street now to block them out, but sometimes a real shithead would just pull them off me so he could try to talk to me. I carried a pepper-foam spray, but when guys like that started into their cat-calling bullshit, I never felt safe.

Hey, baby. Hey, baby. Back that up. You single? He makes you happy? I don't see a ring... Yeah, I love 'em thiiiiiick, baby...lemme get a handful of that... I'd love to take you home and fuck you hard...

Hey, why don't you want to talk to me? You stuck-up or something? Bitch. Whore! Fat ass, you ain't even hot, I was just being nice! I should kick your ass!

Geez, lady, why you so nervous? Not all guys are bad. Though, if they say shit, well, you can't really blame them when you've got those great titties— Hey, where are you going? You frigid or something?

I would have learned to laugh at them were it not for their potential for violence. So far, I had just endured headphone grabs and a beer bottle thrown my way, but I knew a lot of women who had not been so lucky.

For a while, I had almost stopped running because I was so bothered by the harassment —and potential for worse. But it had been a favorite exercise of mine since I started jogging with my dad at the age of twelve, and I really didn't want to give it up.

So, I deliberately dressed down, covered my hair, and kept moving, knowing I would attract less attention that way. And four mornings a week, I went for kickboxing lessons at the local Y... just in case.

Locking the door, I bounded across the lobby and out of the complex, a concrete and stucco filing cabinet of a building that loomed eight stories over the street. My home for four years, paid for with my parents' life insurance. I had lost them in my sophomore year of college, and one of my million regrets about losing them was that I had never been able to show off my very first apartment to them.

I gazed up at it for a moment, before putting in my headphones, turning, and striding down the sidewalk toward Central Park. The Park was my favorite place for a run, and I was eager to spend some time clearing my head as I made a few loops around the reservoir.

I had more than earned the time at work today, that was for certain. As a first-year intern at the *New York Times*, I was constantly swamped—paperwork, filing, copying, office errands, helping to cover the phones...anything but writing or editing news articles.

I knew this dues-paying was part of the process of breaking in to the business, but all the drudgery took its toll after a while. I just wanted to write my own stories for once, but I knew I still had a lot of hard work ahead of me before I would ever get the opportunity.

The most famous publication in the American newspaper business had no room for whiners or slackers. So, every day, I worked my ass off, came home, took a run and a shower, and spent the rest of my night unwinding. Alone, usually. But, again, who had time to date?

My steps against the sidewalk kept a good tempo to the Lenny Kravitz playing through my earphones. As I entered the park, I reluctantly turned off my music, wrapping the earphones around my phone and tucking it deep into my hoodie's kangaroo pocket. I preferred to keep my ears open to the world around me once I reached the park, with its shadowy spots and deserted stretches.

I had only ever been mugged once, and he had left in disgust after discovering I was a penniless college student. Still, the run-in had taught me a serious lesson about being cautious. I had been lucky. The city could chew up and spit out a girl on her own like me if she wasn't careful.

Dangerous or not, I could still enjoy my time here. The night was perfect. Probably forty-five degrees and barely a need for my gloves. The moon hanging overhead was a clear, bright disc with no clouds to block it. I smiled to myself as I jogged over to the reservoir.

I had made half a circuit around that placid artificial lake when I started to realize something strange. New York never slept, the park was open until well past midnight, and yet I had not run into a single person since I entered the grounds.

"That's strange," I murmured quietly.

Where is everyone?

I ran on, keeping an eye out for any other people. Still nothing...a solid mile and a half that, except for me, was completely deserted. The wind had died, and the reservoir's water was as still as black glass under the moon. A dog barked in the distance, and I could hear traffic noises and the high wail of a police siren. But the park itself was as static as a painting. Even the crickets were silent.

About then, I noticed something strange on the dormant grass at the edge of the path. It was an irregular splotch, darker than the rest, the shape vaguely humanoid. As I slowly jogged past it, I realized it was a singed patch on the grass—as if someone's shadow had been burned into the lawn.

I was puzzling over it when a shock went through me. *I'm being watched.* The gut feeling made the hair on the back of my neck stand on end. My breath quickened. I stumbled to a stop and started looking around, trying to pinpoint the cause of this strange, hunted feeling. I saw nothing. But the feeling was getting worse by the second.

Get out of here. Get out of the park.

I could see a gate entrance between the trees a block away, and I made for it, breaking into a sprint. Whatever was going on in Central Park tonight, I wanted nothing to do with it.

I was ten paces from the gate when a shaft of hard white light broke over me like a spotlight. It felt like being hit with a sledgehammer. My muscles locked, and instead of falling, I was yanked upward suddenly, my feet leaving the ground.

For a moment, I stared helplessly out at the darkened, deserted park, smelling the dead grass burning under me, my heart pounding in my ears. *Help,* I thought, mind all but blank with terror. *Someone help me.* But I couldn't speak.

Then the light tore me into pieces.

<hr>

I awoke feeling very groggy. My muscles ached. It felt like I had slept wrong the entire night, and my mattress felt thin and hard for some reason. My whole body was sluggish, like I was suffering from a hangover.

How much of that Chianti did I drink last night?

I lay there rubbing my temples for a few moments before opening my eyes.

It's too damn bright.

The glaring lights forced me to close my eyelids again as pain shot through my head, making me gasp. I waited a moment before opening them again, this time in increments, allowing my eyes to adjust. Once my vision fully returned, my eyes grew wide in surprise.

What the hell? Where am I?

I was lying on my back on a thin, narrow mattress, barely more padded than the soles of my sneakers. The floor beneath it was some smooth gray metal, faintly warm to the touch. My body felt strange, a little bit too light, as if someone had turned gravity down a notch.

It looked as if I was in some sort of cargo hold, though I couldn't feel waves rocking it under me, so maybe I wasn't on a ship. But if it was a warehouse on land, why were the walls metal?

All around me, large, brightly colored containers had been stacked up, sometimes to the ceiling, and bolted together with heavy, dark metal brackets. Their corners had small but powerful lights attached to them, which threw a hard, bluish glow over everything.

To my shock, I saw a few more women huddled on the floor nearby. There were four of them, all of them white and wearing fall-weight clothes. They all looked both hungover and scared, and each one sat on her sleeping mat as if afraid to move from it.

What the hell is going on?

Quickly, I tried to get up, but I ended up banging my head on something. I looked up, blinking, and saw nothing but open air around me. I reached up tentatively and felt a barrier, invisible to the eye but as solid as a wall of heavy glass.

Horrified, I swung my hands around and found my fingertips contacting another solid wall about a foot away from each side of my sleeping mat. I was in the human equivalent of a dog crate—only one with invisible walls.

My heart hammered in my chest as my whole body shook, jolts of adrenaline running through me. *I've been kidnapped.* I remembered the light that had speared down, paralyzing me, lifting me, burning my shadow into the grass before pulling me apart. I had lost consciousness. Now I was whole and here... but trapped, along with the others.

I looked over at the nearest one, a doe-eyed blonde with a thin face and a heavy gray alpaca shawl. "Hey!" I hissed to her. She glanced my way but kept her head down, expression going even more nervous. "Hey. Over here! Can you hear me?" I called again softly. She looked up at me, then around, nodding distractedly. *Oh, thank God.* "Where are we?"

She opened her mouth to speak, but then suddenly looked up and went white as a sheet. Her mouth snapped shut, and she shook her head quickly and put her finger over her lips.

What is going on? "Damn it!" I slammed my palms against the invisible walls keeping me trapped, head pounding in frustration and confusion. But then I noticed something about my fellow captives that shocked me into silence.

On the sides of their necks, right under and behind their ears, a small, bright red light blinked every few seconds. It was round, about the size of a dime, and each one blinked in time with the others. *Marked,* I thought with growing horror. *They have been tagged like animals in a wildlife survey. Or maybe new pets being chipped...*

Cautiously, I reached up, feeling my own neck. *Oh God.* My whole body tensed as I felt a small, round disc embedded under my skin. I let my hand drop, numb with shock. "Fuck," I muttered under my breath.

Who the hell has us? Who has technology like this? The government? The Chinese? Who? I felt all over the walls of my invisible cage, searching for a seam or any weakness. Nothing.

I heard a weird slithering sound coming from somewhere nearby and looked around, but I couldn't see its source. Whatever it was made the other captives nervous.

Maybe I had lived in New York for too long, but when I got nervous, I got belligerent. Nothing made sense, and the only way I was going to get answers was by making some noise. I moved onto my knees and started to thump against the walls of my containment unit. "Hey! Let me the fuck out of this thing!"

I heard a tapping sound and looked over to see the blonde staring at me earnestly. She shook her head several times, and I saw a bruise developing on the side of her face. *What the hell?* I went quiet and realized that the slithering sound was growing closer, accompanied now by a thin, electronic whine.

My head swiveled to look as I caught sight

of a large silver vehicle rounding the corner of one of the stacks of shipping containers. It looked like the upper part of a speedboat, just a cockpit, with walls and a control yoke in front, gliding along on a flat bottom. The floor vibrated slightly as it came nearer...and I caught sight of what was riding in it.

My heart started hammering, and a deep chill ran through my whole body as I got my first good look at my captors. Not military. Not Chinese. Not even human.

They were huge, each one about eight feet tall, but hunkered over, their burly, long-armed bodies reminding me of hairless gorillas. Their skin had a grayish-blue tinge like three-day-old bruises and was leathery-looking and covered in ropy veins.

Their faces were flat, noses mere bumps above single nostrils, and eyes small and black. Sparse manes of stiff, whitish hair grew around the edges of their faces, some of them decorated with beads carved from what looked like bone. Their ears were just holes in the sides of their heads, covered with membranes, like lizard ears. One was missing an eye and had a metal plate bolted to his skull over the socket.

They wore an assortment of beaded jewelry and belts hung with pouches, but were otherwise nude. And male. *Very, very male. Holy fuck.* I got an eyeful of gray dangly bits roughly the size and dimension of baby elephants' trunks before tearing my horrified gaze away.

Aliens. Those are aliens. Those are actual, extraterrestrial, high-tech, intelligent non-humans, and they've kidnapped all of us. I sat there with my heart pounding as I struggled to digest this fact.

There were four in all, drawn by the noise I had made. They peered at me curiously as their vehicle glided up to my cage. I stiffened with fear as the aliens disembarked and walked over to surround my invisible prison.

"Who...are you?" I asked almost breathlessly as I stared out at them. Frustration gave me a touch of courage. "What the fuck is going on?"

Then the aliens did something that scared me even more. A dry, rattling sound escaped from one of them, blooming up into a low hooting with a familiar cadence. The others joined in as they leered in at me, and I started to shake again as I realized what the noise was.

They were laughing.

***

Grab GALAXY ALIEN WARRIORS right now.

WANT FREE SEDONA VENEZ BOOKS?

Sign up for Sedona Venez's Newsletter and receive FREE BOOKS. In addition to the free stories, you will also get special pricing, exclusive previews and news of new releases.

GET A FREE SEDONA VENEZ BOOK!

Join Sedona's mailing list to be the first to know of new releases, free books, special prices and other author giveaways.

https://sedonavenez.com/free-book

ABOUT THE AUTHOR

USA TODAY BESTSELLING AUTHOR SEDONA VENEZ lives in New York City with her hot ex-military hubby—hooah—and their fur babies. She loves writing sizzling, sexy intricate stories about strong but broken characters who push limits, overcome their fears and risk it all for love.

Sedona loves to connect with readers!
www.sedonavenez.com

* 9 7 8 1 9 5 0 3 6 4 4 0 4 *